BARE
PLEASURES

LINDSAY EVANS

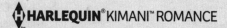

HARLEQUIN® KIMANI™ ROMANCE

Recycling programs
for this product may
not exist in your area.

ISBN-13: 978-0-373-86474-4

Bare Pleasures

Copyright © 2016 by Lindsay Evans

All rights reserved. The reproduction, transmission or utilization of this work in whole or in part in any form by any electronic, mechanical or other means, now known or hereinafter invented, including xerography, photocopying and recording, or in any information storage or retrieval system, is forbidden without written permission. For permission please contact Harlequin Kimani, 225 Duncan Mill Road, Toronto, Ontario M3B 3K9, Canada.

This is a work of fiction. Names, characters, places and incidents are either the product of the author's imagination or are used fictitiously, and any resemblance to actual persons, living or dead, business establishments, events or locales is entirely coincidental.

® and TM are trademarks of Harlequin Enterprises Limited or its corporate affiliates. Trademarks indicated with ® are registered in the United States Patent and Trademark Office, the Canadian Intellectual Property Office and in other countries.

For questions and comments about the quality of this book please contact us at CustomerService@Harlequin.com.

HARLEQUIN®
www.Harlequin.com

Printed in U.S.A.

Lindsay Evans was born in Jamaica and currently lives and writes in Atlanta, Georgia, where she's constantly on the hunt for inspiration, club in hand. She loves good food and romance and would happily travel to the ends of the earth for both. Find out more at www.lindsayevanswrites.com.

Books by Lindsay Evans

Harlequin Kimani Romance

Pleasure Under the Sun
Sultry Pleasure
Snowy Mountain Nights
Affair of Pleasure
Untamed Love
Bare Pleasures

Visit the Author Profile page at
Harlequin.com for more titles.

For my readers, old and new. Thank you.

Chapter 1

Alexander Diallo was taking a break from casual hookups.

He sipped his champagne, his back to the wall of the gallery where his sister was currently having her first solo exhibition, trying not to think how this would impact his social life.

"Hey, Lex." His brother Kingsley walked up with a champagne glass of his own, tapped Lex's glass with it. "Did you congratulate Lola yet?"

"No, not yet. She's a little busy."

In the center of the room, their younger sister stood surrounded by nearly a dozen people. Willowy and petite with big anime eyes her siblings often teased her about, Lola, who was two years younger than Lex, looked years away from being twenty-six. She wore some sort of pale green, flowy dress that brushed the floor, a contrast to her dark and moody paintings on the gallery walls.

"Yeah." Kingsley sipped his champagne and swept his eyes around the rest of the gallery. "A lot of people are here tonight." He said it like he was surprised.

"Why not? She's popular enough and not just on Facebook." Lex tracked his eyes around the room, not so subtly checking out all the gorgeous women not related to him. This resolution wasn't off to a great start.

"Lola is a pretty girl everyone loves to be around, but that doesn't translate to getting people to show up to things that matter," Kingsley said.

An excited squeal caught their attention. Lola had wandered away from her adoring crowd and now stood near one of her more expensive paintings with a long-time friend of the family. A check changed hands.

"Looks like she just sold something," Lex said.

Kingsley nodded. "To one of Mama's friends. Let's hope she can keep selling this stuff once she wears out the family connections. Most of her art-school friends are as broke as she is."

Lex made a deliberately noncommittal noise. His parents were rich. Not as rich as the Kennedys or even Oprah, but they did well enough as owners of a multibillion-dollar cosmetics corporation. Their money, though, was not their children's money, even with the millions held in trust for each and made available after their thirtieth birthdays.

He hated the assumption that just because his parents had a lot of money, that he did too. Over the years, he'd done a lot to distance himself from that belief, from the Diallo Corporation and from money he never earned. Not all his siblings felt the same way; hell, maybe only a couple of them did. Kingsley, the oldest of the thirteen, was their mother's right hand at the company while Wolfe, the second oldest, had built a business of his own from nothing. Or as close to *nothing* as a person can get after borrowing start-up money from their parents.

Lex didn't want any of it. He fought his whole life not to be just another Diallo trust fund kid. He wasn't naive enough to think he was ever truly financially on his own. But what he had, except for the money held in trust, he'd earned for himself.

"What are you doing after this?" Kingsley asked. His champagne glass was now empty and he looked around the gallery with easy hunger. Like Lex would've done a few months or even weeks before, he was on the hunt for feminine distraction. "We're all heading to the bar after the gallery closes."

"I'll come with you," Lex said.

"Good. Maybe you can find a hot girl at the bar to take that frown off your face."

Lex brushed a hand over his face, hoping that gesture, like a mime's trick, would wipe away the frown he hadn't even been aware of. "I'm good," he said. "I'm not having sex these days." The confession rolled smoothly enough off his tongue. He'd practiced saying it out loud.

Kingsley laughed though, a sharp crack that attracted more than a few amused stares. "You all right?"

"Yeah. I'm just not into expending that much energy right now."

His brother looked him up and down, wearing a smile of disbelief. "Maybe expending some...energy is exactly what you need."

"Don't even start," Lex muttered.

His last four relationships had quickly gone south because they got physical way too fast. And after the sex was done, he and the women realized they had nothing left between them. Just sweat and apathy. Those relationships left him feeling emotionally drained and unbalanced. Not that he was looking for meaningful ever-afters, but it all became too much.

"Sex is fun," he said to Kingsley. "But that's not the kind of fun I'm looking for right now."

His brother nodded, looking thoughtful. "But you're okay, right? Nothing wrong with your...?" He waved his hand south of Lex's waist.

"No, man!"

"And it's nothing from before?" Kingsley pressed. Sometimes he took his role as the oldest Diallo sibling a little too seriously.

Still, a mutual memory from ten years ago flared between them. Lex's incessant rebellion had frustrated their parents enough to send him off to Jamaica right after high school. Back then, he'd been the knucklehead son doing the dumbest crap just because he could. Taking his father's car for a joyride. Bringing women into the house to screw when nobody was home. Setting other people's property on fire. Things that infuriated his father and finally made his mother say "enough" in a big way. She sent Lex away to Jamaica for college and to learn better manners. He spent two out of his four years on the island before coming back to America and finishing up at MIT with a degree in electrical engineering and computer science.

"No. Everything's cool," Lex told Kingsley. So far, none of his bad behavior had come back to haunt him.

He took another sip of his champagne and then froze when a flash of long legs caught his eye. Very slowly, so he wouldn't chase away the gorgeous apparition, he lowered his glass to get a better look. High heels. Rounded calves with a hint of muscle. A familiar heat snaked low in his belly and pooled behind his zipper.

He wanted to see more. But when he moved his eyes up to look at the rest of the woman, she disappeared behind a broad back clothed in a pinstripe jacket. Kingsley started to say something the same moment the woman reappeared from behind the pinstripe. She was in profile this time, showing off for him a body like a Coke bottle, thick thighs flowing up into a wide and round ass he easily imagined overflowing his hands. Her waist was ridiculously small. And her breasts… He licked his lips and gave his imagination free rein.

Kingsley waved a hand in front of his eyes, nearly choking with laughter. "Good luck with that celibacy thing."

Lex blinked and took another swallow of champagne to ease the dryness in his throat. "I'm celibate, not blind," he said, still staring at the woman. Her face was pretty in an ordinary way, red lips turned down slightly at the corners, her hair thick and straightened to brush just beneath her collarbones.

"Yeah, well, looking is just the first step. Especially if you're gawking at her like that."

Lex wanted to do more than look. Before his (now ill-advised) vow of celibacy, he'd have walked up to the woman, given her his number and definitely gotten hers. Then they'd probably end up in his bed later that evening. He slid his empty glass on the tray of a passing waiter and deliberately turned away from the woman.

"Well, now I'm not even looking," he said.

"Okay, Lex." Kingsley just laughed at him. What else were big brothers for?

A sharp, brittle sound, cutlery tapping on glass, captured Lex's attention. The gallery's entire focus was moving, conversations halting and flowing into silence to pay attention to Lola, who stood in the center of the room with a champagne glass and a dinner knife in her hands. When the room was quiet enough for her to be heard, she stopped tapping on the glass.

"Thank you all for coming tonight," Lola said. "You have no idea what it means to see you all here celebrating this huge moment with me."

Lex moved closer so he could see her better. His little sister was growing up. Four years out of grad school with her MFA in studio art and a museum job lined up, she was doing very well. Lola had high hopes of making it as an artist but was being responsible and had a backup plan just in case those hopes proved challenging. She was definitely her mother's child, practical while firmly holding on to her dreams. With people from every aspect of her life celebrating her triumph with her, she was glowing. Lex winked when he caught her eye. She giggled in the middle of her speech.

"I couldn't have made it here without the love and support of my family!" Lola grinned and threw her arms wide, nearly splashing the person closest to her with champagne. "I love you all so much!" Her twin, Leo, pushed through the crowd to hug her, his height and wide shoulders just about hiding her from everyone. He kissed her noisily on the cheek, smiling, to the sound of loud whistles and applause.

Lex grinned, proud of how his family stood with

and helped each other. All his brothers and sisters were there to celebrate with Lola. Yeah. She was lucky. They were all fortunate to have each other. An elbow bumped into his and he turned, expecting Kingsley, but it wasn't his brother who he saw. His breath hitched.

No. It can't be her.

The woman who'd caught his attention turned toward the back of the room, but from just the shape of her cheek and chin, the long and narrow lines of her body he knew who it was. Panic dropped, swift and nauseating, into his belly. He stared at the woman, noting the changes from the last time they'd been in the same room. Her face leaner, her clothes more sophisticated and expensive. When she didn't turn back to face him, he began to breathe a little easier.

"You okay, Lex?" Kingsley was suddenly at his side and lightly squeezing his arm. "You look a little gray."

Gray? He felt like all the blood in his body had dropped to his feet, leaving him cold and shaking.

"I'm good." He threw what he hoped was a reassuring smile his brother's way and then turned again to the front of the room, slowing down his breathing. Although he was positive the woman saw him, she never acknowledged him. Maybe she didn't realize who he was. Ten years was a long time. He'd changed a lot since then. His face was thinner, his body less obviously muscular. He'd even grown a couple of inches since those days of being an eighteen-year-old asshole. He took another breath.

"Everything is fine," he said, hoping to convince himself.

When Lola finished her sweet, if disjointed, speech, Lex pushed his way through the crowd to congratulate her. She squealed when she saw him, a tiny whirlwind, and latched her arms around his waist, laughing. Lola smelled like champagne and whipped cream from the bonbons she'd insisted on serving. "I'm so glad you made it! I thought you'd be working again."

Lex had been stuck in front of his computers, either at the office or at home, for most of the past few weeks. The project—fine-tuning a program for national law enforcement to help track, capture and prosecute human traffickers—took up more of his time than he'd initially planned. It kept him from at least one family dinner—he wasn't sure his mother would ever forgive him—and had him regularly estranged from his bed a few nights a week. It was still a work in progress, important work, but there was no way he'd miss Lola's first solo show.

"I *am* working," Lex said. "It's all up here." He tapped his forehead. "I'm great at multitasking."

She clung to his arm, smiling wide to reveal her slightly crooked bottom teeth. "Hmm. That's why you're the smart brother."

"Oh, you do love me." He laughed. Three of their brothers were self-made millionaires and one was on the fast track to NASA. "Get back to your adoring public." He playfully pinched her side and she fell into his chest with an attack of the giggles. "Kingsley and I are waiting to buy you a drink after this is over." He could sense his brother just behind him.

"Okay. But don't run off with some skank before then." She wagged a finger at them both. "Where are these skanks she's talking about?" Kingsley asked, his eyes crinkling with laughter. "It'd be nice to run into a couple right now. I'd even handle your share since you're on lockdown."

Lex made sure to jab a sharp elbow into his brother's side as he passed him and headed to the other end of the gallery where their parents stood together.

"That was rude," Kingsley said loud enough for half the gallery to hear.

Lex ignored him but was grateful for his brother's foolishness and whatever else the two of them would get into before the night was through. He needed a distraction from the woman in the gallery, an unwelcome phantom from his past. He'd have to eventually deal with her and everything she represented. But right now was for celebrating. Right now was for family.

Chapter 2

For Noelle, food was one of the true pleasures of life. She cooked well and often enough to please herself, but when she was someplace that served excellent food or visited a friend who could burn it up in the kitchen, she was in trouble. So she tried to stay away from the food at the gallery opening because it all looked sinfully good. In one of the smaller display alcoves in the back of the gallery, some evil genius had arranged sushi of every conceivable type and color on a model of an old-fashioned Japanese ship. The ship was half Noelle's body length and the rolls were replaced every ten to fifteen minutes. All around the barge, arranged like waves on an ocean, lay golden cream puffs bursting with curls of whipped cream and dusted with powdered sugar.

She tried to stay away from the delicious display but

couldn't. Her sister had dragged her out of her house, and away from Netflix and her pint of pistachio ice cream, to mingle with people she didn't know. Something Margot was doing more often lately. If she had to be away from her extremely comfortable couch, she might as well do something else she enjoyed. Like eat yummy-looking free sushi.

After taking three steps away, Noelle floated back toward the sushi barge. The smell of fresh soy sauce and pickled ginger moved around her like a teasing breeze. She paused to stare at it and then looked away. And saw something else that made her mouth spurt wet with hunger.

What might possibly be the most gorgeous man she'd ever seen stood near the front of the gallery. And he was staring at her. His lips faintly pink and parted. Tongue tucked suggestively into the moist V of the corner of his mouth in a way that made her thighs clench. Noelle frowned and took an unconscious step back at the sudden and ripe desire rising in her to plump her nipples and flutter her pulse. The dip of her spine connected with the sushi table. This man was nowhere near the type who usually caught her eye. She loved the Morris Chestnut types. Dark with silky skin and a six-pack she could scrub clothes on.

This man was nothing like that. He was pretty instead of handsome. Skin like roasted wheat, a slender build and not very tall. He was probably just at her height of five foot eleven. He hovered his mouth over the rim of his champagne and stared at her as if there was no one else in the room.

He stared without giving a damn who was watching him stare. Which was why it surprised her that he caught her attention so completely. He was looking at her, not at her face but at her legs, his compelling gaze gliding up her body in a way that was as thorough as it was intense. He took the champagne glass away from his mouth and licked his lips, a wet swipe of tongue that made her tremble a little, lean back against the table to keep her balance. A man wearing a pinstripe suit walked in front of her, broad and cheerful, saying something about the boat being edible, and rescued her from her disorientation.

Okay. Chill, girl.

She pressed a hand to her belly and turned away from the stranger at the same time the man took another step forward and made a sweeping gesture with his hands. The stranger was still looking at her. She could feel his stare like a hand on her thigh. Unexpected and arousing.

"You okay, Noelle?"

Her sister appeared at her side with a glass bottle of sparkling water in her hand. Slender and tense-looking with her straightened hair styled in a razor-sharp black bob, Margot was dressed in what Noelle called one of her Jessica Pearson suits. A gray couture number tight enough to inspire the proper amount of envy at her slim body, expensive enough to inspire jealousy of her presumably large wallet.

She passed the water to Noelle without asking if she was thirsty. Noelle gratefully took the bottle even as she felt the stranger's eyes slide from her face. Margot was so used to taking care of her since their parents died that it was second nature by now. She gave to Noelle before she took anything for herself. Always looking out for her little sister.

"Thanks." She drank the water, wincing at the effervescence that bit her tongue and throat. "This has been nice, but I think I'm ready to go."

"But we just got here." Margot tucked her handbag more firmly under her arm, instantly looking ready to leave although she obviously wanted to stay. "Lola's about to talk about her artistic process, maybe even invite us to her studio." Margot loved art. If she hadn't been yanked into taking care of Noelle when they were both so young, Noelle imagined that she would've gone to art school too, maybe even had a solo show of her own and been happy. As it was, she didn't think Margot was happy at all.

"It's fine," Margot cut herself off before Noelle could say anything. "We'll leave. I'll take you home after you finish your water."

Earlier that afternoon, Margot had unexpectedly dropped by her house to tell her they had a "sister date." She'd barely given Noelle enough time to put away her ice cream and turn off the television before whisking her off to coffee and then the Wynwood Art Gallery. Another of Margot's constant efforts to get Noelle out of the house.

"I have money for a taxi." She put a hand on her sister's arm. "I know you want to stay." She didn't want to be responsible for Margot giving up yet another thing she enjoyed just for her. Noelle opened her purse to flash a twenty-dollar bill and then a credit card when Margot seemed less than impressed. "I promise I'm not going to be stranded if you stay here and enjoy yourself."

Margot was still as a stone by Noelle's side, her version of indecisiveness. "Please stay. I'll be really sad if you don't."

At the mention of *sad*, a muscle twitched in Margot's jaw. "Are you sure?"

"I'm positive. Stay here and soak up enough culture for both of us." Although she appreciated art as much as the next college graduate, this really wasn't Noelle's scene. She preferred bigger spaces, more adventurous projects. "I'm getting a little headache anyway," she said. "Tell me everything I missed when I see you tomorrow. Okay?"

Margot's agreement came reluctantly. "Okay."

"Good."

Margot hugged her tight, squeezed Noelle like she was about to disappear forever, and then let go with a sigh. "Text me when you get home."

"I will."

She called for an Uber and by the time she walked out into the humid Miami night and down the short flight of steps leading to the sidewalk, a car was already waiting to take her back to her small rented house in Miami Shores. At home, she only made it as far as the couch, where she sank into the comfortably worn cushions and kicked off her shoes.

She tossed her purse on the coffee table, knocking over a bottle of prescription pills. Without looking at them, she knew they were the antidepressants her doctor had prescribed. She was holding off on taking them, not completely convinced that they were what she needed. At least, she hoped not.

Noelle stretched her feet on top of the coffee table, nudging her purse and the pills. The sadness had come over her not too long after her fiancé left her three days before their wedding, tossing her aside with a sorry excuse about needing to find himself somewhere other than married to someone who barely knew herself either. Noelle had thought they were on the same path and would find what they needed together. But she had been wrong.

After seeing her doctor a few days ago, she realized she'd allowed that situation to drag her down to a place she never thought she'd be. A year later, she was thirty pounds heavier and never wanted to leave the house. It shocked her how easily it had happened. And to her, a woman who'd been so independent and self-reliant that she didn't need a man to tell her what she was worth. But here she was, still reeling because his acceptance of her, his adoration, had all been a lie. He hadn't really loved that, at nearly six feet, she was tall enough in high heels to look him in the eyes. He hadn't loved her passion for food and the pleasure she took in eating. He had in no way enjoyed having to coax out her interest in sex.

A brief memory of the man in the gallery jolted through Noelle at the thought of sex. Her body pulsed. Every other thought tumbled away, discarded like clothes on a rushed journey to a bedroom. In the darkness of her living room, she blushed and skimmed a hand across her nipples, which were suddenly achingly hard. She whimpered in pleasure and the sound felt like it came from a stranger. A stranger...

What's wrong with you?

She snatched her hand away from her body and squeezed her eyes shut to rid herself of the memory of him. The here and now was what mattered. He was a beautiful fantasy she needed to wipe from her mind.

But, lying in the dark with her body pulsing dimly for the stranger, Noelle found that was easier said than done.

Chapter 3

A week after the gallery exhibition, Lex still couldn't get the stunning woman out of his mind. At work, he sat in front of his two computer monitors, his mind buried in code until, jolted by his knee, a pencil rolled across his desk, heading for the floor. He caught it. And the smoothness of the pencil between his fingers made him remember the sharp heel of the woman's black shoes, the curve of her foot and the line of her calf.

"Diallo, it's after seven." He flinched when his boss rapped loudly on his door before pushing it open. He squinted at Lex, square hipster glasses magnifying his gray eyes. "Go home!" They were finally in the home-stretch of the project. He could afford to be generous with free time. "Work on it there." Or not. Then he was gone, leaving Lex alone with the pencil still clutched in his hand and his mind still full of *her.*

This celibacy thing was going just great.

After giving his body enough time to calm down, he packed up his work laptop and left the office for the short drive to his house. For the first time in weeks, he was getting home before ten with the project almost finished and his boss well on the way to acting human again. Which made Lex happy. If anyone had asked him ten years ago if he would have felt fulfilled working for a small tech firm in midtown Miami, living in a modest house his parents and most of his siblings could afford with pocket change, he would've said they were crazy. But his contentment came in small packages these days.

When he opened the door, the music he'd programmed to turn on as soon as he walked into the house started playing from the speakers installed in every room. Earth, Wind & Fire's "Boogie Wonderland." At the kitchen counter, he sorted through his mail. Bills. An invitation to a wedding. An envelope with no return address. He frowned and turned it over. The envelope was small and square, just large enough to fit a thank-you note. He slit it open and turned it upside down. A Monopoly card fell to the countertop.

The only thing that surprised him was his lack of surprise.

So she *had* noticed him at the gallery. The card sat on the speckled-gray granite, innocuous-looking but very far from that. It was an old-fashioned "Get Out of Jail Free" card, orange and rectangular. It looked brand-new. Without examining it too closely, he saw that an address was scribbled on the bottom of the card, along with a date and time. Lex closed his eyes and released a slow breath. When he opened them again, he wasn't seeing his own kitchen; instead, he saw the red velvet couches and wide stage of the Kingston strip club where he had hidden from himself for nearly two years, dancing and showing his body off to women who had the money and the time to look.

That time was ten years behind him, but the card brought it back as if it was yesterday.

The date on the card was two days away. A Saturday. He didn't waste his time wondering what she wanted. He left the card on the counter and finished sorting his mail. Saturday would come soon enough.

And it did. When the time came, he dressed like it was any other weekend, in jeans and a T-shirt, pushed his feet in leather sandals and left for the address on the card. It was a small Jamaican restaurant he'd never heard of hidden among the boring beige buildings in Coral Gables. Its outside seating was only two tables on the narrow sidewalk, but that was where he found her.

She sat in a bistro chair facing the road, a too-slender figure in a bloodred suit. The hem of her skirt sliding up above her knees, legs crossed, a black high heel slowly tapping to the music coming from inside the restaurant. She was still as beautiful as he remembered, a brown Morticia Addams, although her hair was short now, styled in a chin-length precision cut. When she saw him, she stood up.

"Alexander."

"Madame M." He felt a little foolish calling her that, but he'd never learned her real name. Not in the two years she had regularly dropped by the club to check on its progress.

A corner of her mouth curled up. "It's good to see

you." She put down the glass of sparkling water she was drinking and reached out to him. Lex clasped her hands in his, a gentle version of a handshake.

"I wish I could say the same," he said.

Her smile faded away. "I understand." She released his hands and sat down. "Please, have a seat. Can I get you something to drink? My treat." She waved the waitress over.

Lex reluctantly smiled. She treated him like the wannabe rent boy he had been ten years ago, offering to spend money on him like he didn't have a perfectly functioning wallet of his own. But what the hell. When the waitress came, he ordered a Red Stripe.

"That's all you want?" she asked.

"For now." Lex thanked the waitress before she left to put in his order.

Then he settled back in his chair, ankles crossed, to wait for the reason Madame M had brought him here. The calm felt good, a direct contrast to the panic that had burned down his spine at the gallery. Back in Jamaica when they first met, he'd been a spoiled and ridiculous kid, high on his own self-importance and spoiling for a fight. He wasn't that dumb kid anymore, but with Madame M in Miami and so close to his parents, who still didn't know about the bad choices he'd made while in Jamaica, he felt antsy.

He drummed his fingers once across the table. "What can I do for you, Madame M?"

She leaned in with a warmish smile on her red lips. "For starters, please, call me Margot."

Margot? The unexpected sweetness of her name almost made him smile. "Okay, Margot. To what do I owe the pleasure?"

"I wish this visit was purely for pleasure," she said.

"I figured it wasn't when you sent the Monopoly card."

She had the grace to look a little embarrassed. "Sorry about that. Sometimes my sense of the dramatic gets the better of me." Her red-tipped fingers curled around the glass of mineral water, but she didn't drink. "By the way, your sister's show was great. I picked up one of her pieces for my living room."

The fact that she had a living room in Miami, or so he assumed, made Lex's hand tingle for the feel of the bottle that hadn't arrived yet. He didn't necessarily want to drink it, but it would give him something to hold on to in his suddenly shifting world.

"I'll let her know you enjoyed it," he said.

Margot chuckled. "Will you really?"

Lex's beer came and he took a long pull from the brown glass bottle. "So, do you plan on telling me anytime soon why you're here?"

"It's actually a little embarrassing—" Her eyebrow jerked up and her mouth quirked, self-deprecating in a way Lex had never seen before. "It's about my sister. And…" She sighed, finally lifting her eyes to meet his. "Just hear me out before you flat out say no."

"If that's not an inviting buildup, I don't know what is," he said.

"I know, right? I think I used to be much better at this."

"Okay." Lex put his beer on the table. Maybe he wanted to be absolutely sober for this. He leaned back in his chair and crossed his hands in his lap. "I'm listening."

"It's my sister," she said again. "She's going through a rough time right now, and I want to help her."

Lex nodded for her to continue, although she obviously didn't need the prompt.

"Her fiancé left her at the altar a year ago." Something moved across her face, an emotion—which was unusual in itself—that Lex couldn't clearly interpret. "She hasn't been the same since. Maybe not depressed, exactly, but close enough that it makes me worry."

It sounded like something normal enough to Lex. If someone he trusted and loved enough to think of settling down with suddenly left him in the lurch with a lifetime of embarrassment and an outfit he couldn't return, he'd hole up at home in his pajamas too.

"Since we were kids, I've been the one to take care of her. I want to take care of this for her too." Her gaze on him sharpened and, if he had been ten years younger, Lex would have quickly excused himself and run like hell. But he sat and waited for what would come out of her mouth next. "This is where you come in," she said.

Either he was getting braver in his older age or stupid. "I don't see any room for myself in this equation," he said carefully. "If you're that worried, get her to see a shrink."

"She's already doing all that, but it's not working. What I want you to do is distract her from her depression."

Lex raised an eyebrow. "I don't think it works like that."

"It can," Margot insisted with a certainty that would've been admirable if she wasn't talking about *manipulating* her sister. "Noelle is depressed right now, not clinically but just having a moment in her life. A distraction like you will be good for her."

Lex didn't bother to ask what she meant by *a distraction like you*. "You think asking one of your ex-strippers to sleep with her will solve her problem?" He ignored the flash of anger in Margot's eyes and pushed on. "I don't mean to be the bearer of bad news, Margot, but this isn't going to go the way you think."

"No, no, no. You are *not* going to sleep with her." Margot shook her head so hard that the ends of her hair slapped her mouth. "I never allowed that in the club and I'm certainly not going to ask you to do that now."

"You want me to seduce her out of her depression but not have sex with her? Sounds like you want her to be pissed off and *more* depressed when this whole thing is over." Just like he would be.

"Noelle has never been a sexual person—wow, I don't even know why I'm telling you this—" Instead of covering her face as it looked like she was going to do, Margot primly clasped her hands on top of the table. "I don't think you teasing without delivering will be a problem."

Her justification for wanting to do this for her sister looked pretty thin. Lex understood about wanting to take care of the people you love, but this...this didn't seem to be the way to go at all.

"Margot, don't think I'm not grateful for what you did for me back in Jamaica, but even you have to see this is a little crazy. Making me into a neutered stud for your sister just because she has a little case of the blues doesn't make sense here. I don't think you'll be doing her any favors. Let her find her own way out of this. I'm sure your sister is more capable than you're giving her credit for." *Especially if she's* your *sister*, Lex silently added.

"I have to do this for her, Alexander. I have to." The emotionless mask she always wore bent at the edges and he could see hints of her desperation, the love she had for her sister and the care she wanted to take of her. "You're just what she needs right now. And I trust you to fulfill those needs without overstepping your boundaries." She raised a meaningful eyebrow, reminding him again that he wasn't allowed to go too far with her sister.

Since he wasn't going to agree to any of her madness, it didn't seem necessary to bring up his current celibacy.

"Margot, even though I hate to say no to you, I have to step back from this. What you're planning doesn't feel right, and it sure as hell doesn't sound necessary."

"Consider it a little longer, Alexander. I'm not asking you for a kidney here."

"That would be easier," he said.

Margot palmed her water again, looked at Lex as if she was seeing him for the first time and then glanced away to the pedestrian traffic parading past.

"You've changed," she said.

"Of course. I'm sure you have too. After all, it's been ten years." He was twenty-eight now. She had to be at least forty.

Her eyes ran a slow course over him, from the top of his head, his hair cut close with tight waves, over his America Eagle jeans, to the simple leather sandals on his feet. "And it's not just the clothes you wear. No latest-designer gear, no pierced nose."

Lex grinned, a quick flash of teeth. "The piercings have moved to more inconspicuous locations." Her eyebrow arched playfully at that. "But I like to think

I've cultivated some more mature tastes in the last few years. For no other reason than to save money. Keeping up with the Kardashians is expensive." He quirked the corner of his mouth.

"You've definitely changed. I didn't exactly expect the same arrogant boy from the club, but…"

"But you did."

"Yes, or at least, I expected to see some remnants of him." Her eyes dipped to the T-shirt draped across his chest, which was no longer swollen with muscle like it had been the last time she saw him. He'd cut down on that too. Less being more and all that.

He said as much.

"Very droll."

"I'm just not as worried about things as I used to be." Then he had to laugh at himself, considering how worked up he'd been when he saw her at the gallery. "Mostly, anyway."

She nodded, finally taking a sip of water that had to be room temperature now. "Well, I hope the man you've become will consider my plea. It's a favor that I'm asking, not a trade, not a bribe. This is just something you're uniquely qualified to do. You're the only man I trust to do what I ask without taking advantage of my sister."

Lex hummed to let her know he was listening, but he had already made his decision. She wasn't blackmailing him, so he could safely say no. Maybe after he refused her for the last time, Margot would get her sister some real help.

"Okay," he said. "I'll think about it."

"That's all I can ask."

Ask all you want, he thought. *I'll still say no.* "Now that that's out of the way, what have you been up to?"

"The same. A little bit of this and that."

He almost laughed again. In Jamaica, he hadn't known much about Margot. Not even her name. She came to the club four to six times a year, trusting the running of its operations to a pair of streetwise twins who made sure nothing illegal happened at the place.

"So things haven't changed for you that much, then," Lex said.

"Well." She drew out the word, obviously reluctant to share any information with him, despite just asking him to seduce her sister. "I sold the club and invested in some less controversial properties."

From conversations he and Margot had toward the end of Lex's time in Jamaica, he knew she'd inherited the club from her parents, who were long dead. She had transformed the slightly sleazy, uptown girly bar into an exclusive, membership strip club that catered to both men and women and had a dedicated ladies' night when men were not allowed. Women paid for the privilege of ogling hard and oiled masculine bodies without men sitting among them. During the rest of the week, the club hosted mostly rich and powerful men in the audience while gorgeous girls of every shade danced on stage or made themselves available for lap dances.

"So you're doing well for yourself here in Miami, then?" Lex asked. Margot's designer suit and thousand-dollar stilettos said as much, but she wouldn't be the first person to floss in haute couture when they were damn near homeless.

"I get by," she murmured.

She was probably a millionaire several times over.

Lex smiled and pushed away his drink. Time to do a little research, then. "I'm glad you're satisfied," he said, feeling far from that state himself. But that would change soon.

His phone vibrated in his front pocket. "Excuse me," he said as he reached for it.

His twin's big eyes flashed at him from the screen. He answered the phone, turning slightly away from Margot. "Hey."

"What are you doing?" Adisa asked the question as if she knew he wasn't doing anything special.

"Nothing much. What's up?"

"You're not getting ready for family dinner tonight?"

"What's to get ready for? I'm dressed and showered. My car is working so I'll be able to drive there."

"You're such an idiot. You do know it's their anniversary, right?"

"I think you're the one being an idiot. I know when their anniversary is and it's not today."

"It's the anniversary of you know…" Her voice trailed off dramatically in typical Adisa fashion.

The *you know* was the unfortunate incident of their parents' separation when their mother ran off to some island with another man. Their parents didn't think they knew, but all the siblings were very aware of what had happened, although not why, and had created an unofficial celebration of their parents' reunion by dropping by their house, even when it wasn't a family dinner, and bringing presents.

With the meeting with Margot on his mind, Lex had actually forgotten. "Okay, fine."

"So, what are you bringing?" Adisa pressed, sounding impatient.

Lex barely stopped himself from saying something mean. "Right now, nothing."

"Let's go shopping and then we can go to the house after. You can even buy me a drink."

"Why am I buying you a drink when you make at least four times my salary?"

"Because you're older and that's what older brothers do."

He was about to remind her that older by twelve minutes didn't really count, but then he remembered where he was. Lex sighed heavily into the phone. "I'll be at your place in fifteen."

"Perfection. I'll be waiting for you on the porch with fresh coffee." They were both caffeine addicts and drank coffee any time of the day or night, especially when they were together.

"French vanilla, please," Lex said.

"Like I don't know who I'm talking to." She hung up.

Lex slid the phone back into his pocket.

"You have to go?" Margot looked amused. She'd never seen him interact with any of his siblings before. Their entire relationship had been in the context of Lex's isolation from his twin and the rest of his immediate family.

"I do have to go." Lex took one last sip of his lukewarm beer. "But I'll be in touch."

She reached across the table to squeeze his hand, her eyes rising to meet his. "I'm looking forward to it."

"Even if I say what you don't want to hear?"

"I'm an optimist," she said.

Lex got to his feet. "All right, Margot. We'll talk

soon." Then he left the restaurant without any intention of ever seeing her again.

When he pulled up to Adisa's front door, she was sitting on her front step reading her version of a trashy novel. On the cover was a pretty illustration of nuclear fission. Like him, she was a nerd from way back.

"Lexie!" She jumped up from the step, slipped her book under her arm and grabbed the two cups of coffee at her side, one with her lipstick stain on its rim. "I swear, you are the most punctual black man in the universe. What did you do, roll out of bed and push her out the door at the same time?"

He unlocked and opened the car door to let her in. "I didn't push anybody anywhere."

"Right. You were with a woman. I know it." She passed him his coffee and climbed into the car butt-first, bringing the smell of vanilla-flavored coffee and her bergamot body lotion, a Diallo Corporation blend, with her. She wore her natural hair pulled back from her face and circled with a bright blue scarf. Jeans, a cropped white T-shirt and a gold body chain that flashed at the neckline of her shirt and across her flat belly completed her latest casual look.

"There was a woman, yeah." He could never hide anything from Adisa, and he never wanted to. "But not that kind."

"A butterface?" She plopped her coffee in the appropriate cup holder and slammed the door shut. "Understandable. You're a pretty devil, but sometimes you gotta take whatever is available."

"Don't be crass."

She tipped her head back in mock shock and then

burst out laughing. "Don't take this all new Alexander to boring levels, brother dear. Remember I knew you back when."

Lex started the car just after she belted herself in, gunning the engine of the Charger and taking off so fast that she slammed back into her seat.

Adisa grabbed the door handle. "You asshole!" But she was laughing. "Wait until I tell Mom…"

Chapter 4

Working on Saturdays is for suckers, Noelle thought. Which made her the biggest sucker of all since this was the third Saturday in a row she was in the office. She worked the extra hours for no reason other than she wanted to finish the work on a pending case that her boss needed ASAP.

"Fuck my life," she muttered as she stepped outside the law firm's five-story building into the sunshine and eighty-degree heat.

It was a gorgeous fall day with just the right amount of crispness in the late morning to make her long for a walk to her favorite Cuban bakery for a *pastelito* and then a stroll back home to savor that hint of cool weather that Miami got blessed with once in a blue moon. But instead of doing that, she'd been at work. Researching, collating that research and sending it off to her boss in a format he could understand.

Noelle shrugged out of her sweater and draped it over her arm, slid on her sunglasses and walked toward her car. A few feet away from her little red Honda Civic, she stopped mentally complaining for long enough to realize there was somebody leaning on her car.

"Hey, there." Margot waved her phone at her. "I was just about to text you."

"How did you know that I was here?"

"You told me you were catching up on some work, remember?"

Noelle searched her memory but couldn't find such a conversation. But she shrugged. "Okay. What's going on?"

"I'm taking you out to lunch."

Noelle looked at her watch and saw it was just past eleven o'clock. She'd been in the office since eight.

"Come on. I'm parked over there."

Margot gestured toward her own car, a black four-door Mercedes parked in the shade.

Noelle was never one to turn down a free meal. "Okay. Let me just switch out these heels for my flip-flops." She'd gotten dressed for the office, just in case someone else happened to come in. The professional suit and high heels were comfortable in the office, but now that she was off and on her own time, she felt like putting on sweats and sneakers.

"No, you should keep on your shoes," Margot said. "Let's go."

Oh. That meant they were going someplace fancy. With small portions. Lord help her.

"All right." Noelle suppressed a sigh, hitched her purse more securely on her shoulder and walked with her sister to her car. The Mercedes still smelled new after nearly a year. The interior was as clean and organized as if Margot had just driven it off the lot. Noelle settled in beside her sister and let Margot sweep her away to parts unknown.

Parts unknown turned out to be a restaurant in Key Biscayne. Four stars, without listed prices and with a sommelier on staff, according to the menu. Noelle secured her bag under the table with a purse hook and wriggled herself to comfort in the plush chair. Leather and wood cupped her back like the hands of a lover, tucking her sweetly up to the table.

"This is a nice place," she felt obliged to say.

She loved her sister and had known her all her life, so she sensed Margot was up to something. Noelle waited for it, ordering an appetizer and glass of pomegranate juice in the meantime. Margot looked like she was coming from a meeting, wearing one of her obvious power suits with a pair of those red-bottomed shoes she loved so much. She appeared commanding and cold; a look she deliberately cultivated. Sometimes Noelle missed the sister she'd known before their parents left their lives. The sister who played made-up games with her and loved to push her in shopping carts through store parking lots until they were both giggling from the rush.

Noelle sipped her juice and made small talk with Margot, sneaking peeks at her watch and waiting.

Then finally Margot said, "This place is nice, right?"

Noelle let out a breath she didn't realize she'd been holding. "Yeah," she said. "This is good." She raised her glass of bright red juice, served in a wineglass with a lemon peel curled on the edge and a sprinkling of pomegranate seeds at the bottom.

The waiter came then, properly dressed in his dark apron, and presented their appetizers on tiny plates. He was gone so fast it was as if he disappeared into thin air. This was the kind of service Margot liked. Efficient and just about invisible. Noelle picked up her fork and prepared to demolish the prettily presented crab cakes, determined to at least get Margot's money's worth before her sister ruined her appetite.

"This is a nice place," Margot said again, picking through the sparse leaves of her starter salad with a fork that looked like real silver. "It's nice to be able to afford a place like this, don't you think so?" She ate her salad without dressing and tipped her head to look at Noelle with what Margot seemed to think was her most inscrutable expression.

But Noelle had known Margot long enough to read nearly everything about her. Right now, the slight upward curve of her mouth, the minute quiver of her eyelashes said she was feeling pleased with herself about something. In other people's company, she laughed often, sometimes even reached out to touch in a show of closeness and connection. When she was being herself, though, she was contained. Barely there smiles instead of laughs, hands still and clasped close to her body. Their parents' abandonment and then death had changed them both.

"Yes," Noelle agreed. "It's nice you can afford this place and treat me to lunch." Although she knew that wasn't the point, Noelle added, "Thanks for inviting me out today."

"You know it's nothing. Anytime I can take my little

sister out is a good day." Margot twirled her fork in a pile of spinach leaves like it was spaghetti.

"I could take you out to a place like this if that's what you really want," Noelle said. "But you'd have to wait until payday."

"That's just my point." Margot's eyes snapped with triumph, a subtle shimmering under her thick fan of lashes, the only thing about her that was lush. "Wouldn't you love to take yourself out for meals like this whenever you want? Without worrying about a paycheck or making payments toward it on your credit card?"

Noelle shrugged, forked off another piece of crab cake in her mouth—and it practically melted there, buttery and faintly sweet—before she said anything. She slowly chewed, savoring the crab meat on her tongue. "I have the kind of life that I want, Margot. You know that. Eating at expensive places and wearing shoes that cost as much as one month's rent is not my thing. It's yours."

Noelle put another piece of the tiny crab cake in her mouth, determined to enjoy every last bite while she could.

"If you ever used any of the money in your inheritance account, you'd want that too."

Noelle rolled her eyes. Some random nightclub in Jamaica their parents had owned started to actually turn a profit a few years after Margot took over. Her sister made sure Noelle's share of the profits got deposited into an account they both referred to as the *inheritance account*. Noelle knew the money was there and knew it was a *lot* of money, but she rarely looked at it, preferring to leave it there for the rainy day that life with her parents taught her was always coming.

"*If* is a big word, Margot. Right now, I have everything I need and can buy everything I want." That wasn't quite true. She couldn't afford to take the trip to the Great Barrier Reef she wanted, but that was only a matter of saving her vacation time.

"But what if you just went to law school and became an entertainment lawyer? Wouldn't that be better than just being a paralegal at the firm? You could work directly with ball players and entertainers as their legal counsel."

It was an old conversation but framed in a different way. Margot had money. Noelle didn't know exactly how much and she didn't care. Just like she didn't care about the details of the inheritance account, it was simply enough to know Margot had financial security. Her sister had given up her own childhood to make Noelle comfortable when their parents disappeared for the last time. Noelle was nine. Margot was nineteen. When the disappearance ended with Hugo and Michelle Palmer being found dead on some abandoned farm in the middle of Iowa, the girls breathed a sigh of relief. Not because they were rid of their parents, but because they finally knew where they stood. Alone.

Margot dropped out of college and took over running the Jamaican nightclub, taking care of Noelle every day except for the half a dozen times each year she left the country to check on the club and other businesses she had going. Other than during those disappearances, when Margot left Noelle with a trusted friend of their mother, Margot was there to make her meals, help with homework and provide every material thing they needed. Margot had sacrificed to get the money and financial freedom she had now. But that was not what Noelle wanted for herself. Her small happiness was more important to her than any pair of thousand-dollar shoes or meals that cost a hundred dollars a plate.

The waiter came back to take away empty dishes and bring their entrees, but Noelle didn't pick up her fork.

"I already told you, Margot, I like my life the way it is. When I'm not at the office, I don't have to worry about anything there unless I feel like it. Most of the lawyers work through lunch and miss dinner with their families and spend entire weekends at the office instead of being with the people they love. I don't want that."

"Even if I pay for the LSATs and law school for you?"

That was a new one. Margot had offered to pay for the LSATs before but never for law school. Noelle took her napkin out of her lap and lay it across the table. Carefully, she rested her hands on either side of her plate and drew a calming breath.

"I don't want to sound ungrateful about this, Margot. But if you don't stop harping on this law school thing, I swear to God I'm going to walk out of here and take the bus back to my car."

Margot sighed and sat back in her chair. "Calm down. I'm not trying to upset you. I'm just—"

"I know what you're *just* trying to do, Margot. But we're not our parents. I'm not completely broke and reliant on a man who takes chances with my life. You're not a drug-addicted gambler who can't tell a trap from a score." She swallowed the sudden tears that threatened the back of her throat. "And we're not kids anymore and I can make my own decisions about the kind of life that I want." Noelle took another breath and truly tried to calm herself down. Their parents had done a number on them both, especially Margot, who thought she had to fix everything in Noelle's life. Hell, she'd wanted to fix her anger at Eric for jilting her by hiring someone to break his legs.

For a moment, it looked like Margot's carefully constructed facade was going to crack, like she was finally listening to what Noelle was saying and actually understood. But then she picked up her fork and knife as if Noelle hadn't spoken.

"Fine," she said. "We'll let this conversation go for now. Just know that I love you." Margot swallowed loudly. "And I only want the best for you."

"I know." Noelle hooked her bottom lip between her teeth. That was what made it so hard for her to be truly angry at her sister. She did it all out of love and fear that they would both slide to where their parents had been. No matter what Noelle said or did, she couldn't convince Margot they were okay. She blew out a breath and reached for her fork.

"It's okay, Mags. Just eat your food before it gets cold."

Margot gave her a smile that was only a painful stretch of teeth. But it was better than nothing. Noelle drank some of her fruit juice and tried to settle the knots in her stomach. It didn't quite work, but it was a start.

Chapter 5

"I don't know how you actually grew up in this family and never learned how to cook." Alice Diallo turned around at the massive kitchen island and passed Lex the platter of fried dumplings she'd made that afternoon.

The entire house buzzed with the presence of thirteen Diallo children, their parents, partners and a few close friends. Dinner was due to start in less than fifteen minutes. Everyone was there and accounted for, the large house humming with music and conversation, laughter from the big verandah, the living room and the dining room. Lex had been drafted to help set the table since he didn't cook.

"I'm a decent-enough cook," he told his sister as he left the kitchen, "I just don't want to cook for your greedy asses. You might get used to it and ask me to do it on the regular." His sister made a rude noise.

Lex placed the covered platter in the middle of the table along with all the other prepared dishes. Unlike official, quarterly family dinners when their mother either cooked or had the meal catered, this time each of the Diallo children brought a dish to share. Lex brought sorrel from his backyard, a potent mixture he planted, harvested and made himself that had plenty of white rum and was not fit for the children's consumption. There was already wine, but Lex put the sorrel—stored in Red Label bottles—in champagne buckets on both sides of the table.

"It's almost time to eat!" he called out. He'd barely finished yelling when his siblings started flooding into the room.

But he noticed that his parents weren't among them. "Hey, where are Mama and Daddy?"

"You know better than to ask that question," Kingsley said, sitting next to their youngest sibling, Elia.

Wolfe, the second oldest, gave Lex a laughing look. "Probably in their room. I doubt you want to go find them. They'll come down when they're ready."

But Alice poked him in the side with a naughty grin. "Go get them. Tell them Elia better be the last one. We don't need another kid running around here."

"Hey! I'm not a kid." Elia piped up. "I'll be eighteen in, like, three weeks."

"Oh wow…so mature."

The room exploded in laughter before Lex could see who'd spoken. Most of the seats were already taken. It didn't seem right for his parents not to be there.

"I'll be right back," he said.

"Don't say we didn't warn you!" Wolfe called out as Lex walked away.

But he knew they weren't in their room. He'd seen them in the den earlier after giving them their unofficial anniversary present: a digital picture frame with all the kids' photos preloaded. Upstairs, as he walked closer to the den, he heard their voices, low and intimate. He paused. Maybe Wolfe was right. But the den's door wasn't closed. Even in their own house, they wouldn't fool around with the door wide open for anyone to walk in and see.

"This is really something," his father was saying.

"Sometimes I can't believe it's the same boy." His mother's voice was muffled and soft.

When Lex got close enough, he saw them standing near his father's desk looking at the pictures scrolling by in the digital frame. His mother was resting her head against her husband's chest.

It was a running joke among the Diallo children that their parents were always screwing like rabbits, that it was a lucky thing they'd only ended up with thirteen kids instead of thirty. Lex started to turn around and leave them to their privacy, but they shifted apart and his mother called out.

"Alexander?"

He turned back toward the den, his fingers resting lightly on the wall. "Yes, it's me," he said. "Dinner's ready."

His mother came toward him, just as his father met his eyes with a smile before looking back at his wife. "I told you we were going to be late if you kept up your sentimental tripe."

Lex grinned. Of the two, his father was the more sentimental and likely to break down in tears. But only in the presence of family.

His mother, graceful and elegant even in jeans and a screen-printed shirt that Elia had given her for their unofficial anniversary, slid her fingers between his.

"Thank you for the gift, Alexander. It's wonderful." She smelled of coffee and bitter chocolate still, remnants of earlier that evening when she and his father had been exiled to a nearby coffee shop so the kids could take care of dinner.

"You're welcome, Mama."

His father came up behind her, looming tall and distinguished in the new gray-flecked goatee he'd been trying out for the last few weeks. "Although we don't say it nearly enough, we're very proud of you." He shared a look with his wife and Lex wondered where this was coming from. Then he remembered the photos he'd uploaded in the frame, especially the ones of him as a teenager smirking at the camera, looking like he was on the hunt for trouble. "The success you made for yourself," his father continued. "The peace you found once you came back to us whole and settled all those years ago." He was talking about Jamaica, the end of Lex's rebellious phase. And Lex couldn't help but think about Margot and the role she had in that.

"You came back to us better than we ever dreamed," his mother said. "We're so happy you made it." Unspoken was the reality that he could very easily have burned himself out and ended up hurt or worse.

His father rested a hand on his shoulder, a light and loving weight. "Very happy."

Lex squeezed his father's hand and swallowed the lump of emotion in his throat. "I...just came to call you for dinner." He cleared his throat, cursing the tremor in his voice. "Don't let the food get cold." Then he turned and left them before they could see the wetness in his eyes.

He'd come a long way since he was eighteen and breaking his parents' hearts with just about every decision he made. It had taken a conversation or eight with Madame M—with Margot—to make him realize what he was turning his back on. Family. The people who loved him unconditionally even when they were tired of his mess and trying to help him clean it all up.

Downstairs, Lex turned into the first room he came to: his mother's office. With the smell of his mother's fragrance around him—his mother who'd never cried but clung to him like he was a precious thing she had almost lost—Lex fumbled for his phone. He brought up Margot's number and, after a moment's hesitation, sent her a text.

I'll do it.

Soft conversation rippled through the tea shop where Lex stood. He lurked near the intimidating wall of loose-leaf tea selections, trying to decide what he was in the mood for. The display of teas was impressively large. He wanted to bury his nose in every single metal container and inhale their particular scent until he could decide what it was that he actually wanted. It also helped him to stall and wait for what he was really at the tea shop for.

It wasn't long before his patience was rewarded and Margot walked in. She pushed open the door, talking with a woman who came in just behind her, a woman whose face Lex couldn't immediately see. There was something familiar about her body though, lushly made with high yet heavy breasts covered in a gray V-necked T-shirt and a cascade of tiny gold chains, hips that curved sweetly under blue jeans and made something low in his belly jerk to attention. Maybe she was an actress from a movie or television show he'd seen once. Then he saw her face.

Lex's hand brushed one of the tins of loose-leaf tea, and the tea tumbled off the shelf, spilling golden chamomile flowers all over the tile floor. He winced when every eye in the place, including Margot's, swung to him. He was certain he saw her amused gaze before she turned back to the woman with her, her sister. The same woman he'd seen at the gallery. The universe was either seriously messing with him or giving him a gift straight from heaven.

He tore his eyes away from the woman and dropped to one knee to gather the spilled chamomile the same moment someone came from behind the counter with a small broom and dustbin. Lex apologized for the mess while the man waved him away with a smile, saying something about accidents happening all the time. But although Lex was trying his best to deal with the tea and man and the sudden gallop of his pulse, his attention was still firmly focused on Margot's sister.

Only two weeks had passed since he saw her, but his body jerked tight and grew warm like it was only yesterday that it had hardened for her. As his body reacted to her presence, Lex felt like he was on display, the priapic man unable to control his reaction to a seductive woman walking into a place where he'd expected duty, only to be faced with desire. He shook his head at his own dramatics and backed away from the tea display and the guy with the broom before he could do any more damage.

After ordering a smoothie, he stood to the side and watched the two women while trying not to be obvious about it. The only features the two women shared were their above-average height and nut-brown skin. Otherwise, they were night and day. Margot was so beautiful and strikingly slender that, if Lex hadn't known her, he'd have thought she'd just stepped off the plane from a fashion show in Milan. Her smiles were wide and inviting, but there was no warmth in them. Her sister, though, was…all heat and invitation, even though she wasn't smiling. Objectively, her face was pretty enough, but there was nothing in it to inspire a league of Instagram followers. Square-ish jaw. Long-lashed eyes. A full and slightly downturned mouth. He very deliberately did not look any lower than her chin.

The sisters stood at the back of the line without paying him the slightest bit of attention. Which he was grateful for. Soon enough, they stepped past him, Margot's sister saying in a soft voice what teas she liked. Margot only said a few words until they were at the front of the line, where she ordered tea service for two and two curry-chicken sandwiches. Once their order was placed, they sat an empty table to wait. That was Lex's cue.

He dialed a number and, a few feet away, Margot made a sound of surprise and reached for her own phone. Once she answered, he hung up, but she kept the phone to her ear and said something into it Lex couldn't hear. When she put the phone down, the look on her face was all apology.

"I'm really sorry about this, Noelle, but I have to go."

"What? Now? We already ordered."

Because of her soft voice, Lex had positioned himself to hear her conversation, but then he had to step back from the counter when someone else came up to place their order. Margot apologized again—a little too profusely, it seemed to Lex— and then kissed her sister's cheeks even as Noelle was still sputtering about not wanting to drink a whole pot of tea and eat two sandwiches by herself.

"Why don't you share the service with someone here?" Margot asked. "That way, it won't go to waste." She apologized again before pushing her way out the door. Noelle sat at the table, stunned for a few seconds, and just as she got up, probably to get the order to go, Lex stepped close to her table with his most charming smile.

Damn, she was even sexier up close. Her body one curve after delicious curve, her lips glistening with clear gloss.

"Excuse me, miss. I couldn't help but overhear your conversation."

"Didn't your mother tell you not to eavesdrop?" Noelle looked up at him with suspicion and then she blinked, her eyes going wide. Lex felt a surge of satisfaction. She remembered him too. "Oh, hi…" she finished, her voice a little breathless.

"My mother told me a lot of things," Lex said, drowning in her dark-rimmed eyes that shone with just a touch of sadness. "One of them was to always speak to a beautiful woman since you never know if she'll be the mother to your babies." He hoped his mother would forgive him the lie. Any advice about women she'd given him had always been about wearing raincoats and not every date being a keeper. He widened his smile.

"Your mother sounds very optimistic," Noelle said. She bit her lip and skipped her eyes over his body, a quick and burning look he remembered well from the night at the gallery.

"She is," he said. "Very."

The sun arched through the glass front of the tea shop and fell into the arc of Noelle's throat, down the sumptuous line of her chest, glinting in the fall of tiny necklaces. Gold on top of gold. "I've seen you before," she said.

"And I've seen *you*." Lex allowed a trace of what he'd felt that night at the gallery to show in his face, the instant attraction and honest lust. Noelle bit her lip again and her eyes fluttered low, an answering desire flowing like water over her face. That naked passion gave Lex the encouragement to continue. "Like I was about to say before being unfairly interrupted, do you mind if I join you?"

Noelle dipped her head and her shoulder-length hair, straightened and glossy, shifted over her shoulders. When she looked back up at Lex, the bloom of sexual interest had disappeared like she had put that part of herself behind a door and firmly locked it away. "As much as I would enjoy your company," she said, "I have to go." Her face was a study in conflicting emotions.

She made the motion to stand up and Lex acted quickly, spurred by desperation. It wasn't about Margot and what she wanted anymore. This was the woman who had haunted his dreams and fed his fantasies for the past fourteen nights. He *needed* her to stay with him. "If you leave now, you'll never experience the best thing you've ever had in your mouth."

She leaned away from him. "Excuse me?"

"The taro smoothie they serve here. It's really good." He teased her with a smile. "Why? What did you think I meant?"

She blinked up at him in surprise and a hint of a smile touched her lips. Just then, one of the guys from behind the counter appeared with a tray holding the sandwiches and pot of tea.

"Here you are, ma'am." He settled Noelle's order on the small table and then, after making sure she had everything, took her ticket. Noelle thanked him before he disappeared back behind the counter.

She stared down at the carefully arranged tea and sandwiches like she didn't know what to do with it all.

Lex reached across the table and offered her his hand. "I'm Lex."

"And you're very persistent."

"But hopefully not a pest." He wanted this to be the moment they connected, but he wasn't going to force it if she really wasn't feeling him. He knew the power of his charm, but he also knew its limits.

Noelle tipped her head to look up at him, the smooth tumble of her hair sliding over her shoulders in a way that made him long to tug it firmly until her throat was bare to him and she was gasping for his touch. "You're not a pest yet," she said, oblivious to his slow but steady burn.

Lex widened his thighs under the table, making room in his pants for his growing…problem. He released a silent breath and turned his attention to the tea and sandwiches in front of them. "That looks good,"

Lex murmured. "I'll share it with you if you share my taro smoothie with me."

She still seemed undecided, like at any moment she would shove away from the table and bolt. Lex made the decision for her. He poured a cup of tea for her and one for himself. The tea, fragrant with ginger and chamomile, steamed against his face, the same tea he'd scattered all over the floor earlier. "So what happened back there? Your girlfriend bail on you?"

He smiled with relief when Noelle only looked amused as he sipped the tea. Her internal shrug, just before she reached for her own teacup, was almost comically obvious. "Margot isn't my girlfriend, although she can be as overbearing as the worst kind of wife." She tilted her head, her forehead wrinkling. "I'm actually a little surprised she just left me here. Half the time I swear she thinks I'm some naïf wandering through the deep, dark woods about to stumble into danger at every turn."

Naïf. Lex smiled at the word. He had the sneaking suspicion that Margot's opinion of her sister's proximity to suicidal cliff jumping was very far from reality.

"I'm sure you'll set her straight soon enough." Lex took another sip of the tea and nodded in approval. "This is good. I've never tried this blend before."

"You come here a lot?"

He grinned. "You're asking if I come here often."

"Oh my God. Your ego is large, isn't it?"

She was perfect, really. Lex chuckled. "Not my ego, no."

Her lips twitched again. She was restrained, even in her amusement. It made him want to pull out all the stops to make her laugh, even make a fool of himself if that was what it took.

"Sir, your taro smoothie." A young girl appeared at Lex's shoulder. He thanked her and took the tall glass, which was filled to the top with the lavender smoothie and had boba resting like dark pearls at the bottom.

Once the girl left, he slid his glass across the table toward Noelle. "Try this. Your mouth will thank you."

She shook her head. "In a minute. I'm not sure I'm ready for a mouth-changing experience." She held the tea under her nose, steaming her face with the fragrant blend and closed her eyes for a moment. "This is what I came here for. I've been trying to convince Margot to come here forever. Then the day I finally get her to come, she gets called away on a mystery errand." She sipped her tea, and the taste of it on her tongue seemed to make her smile. "Figures."

"Well, it's my lucky day," Lex said. He reached for one of the sandwiches and took a big bite. "Mmm. Definitely my lucky day." And he made sure he conveyed with his eyes just what part of the day's good fortune he was truly grateful for. "Thank you."

"You're welcome," she said, after swallowing her tea. "I think. I'm not really into being considered a prize in this scenario."

"Not a prize. Just interesting company for a guy who'd otherwise be having a lonely day."

He suspected an admission of loneliness might resonate with her and make her open up to him in a way that bold flirtation wouldn't. Deliberately, he did *not* think about just how else he wanted her to open up for him.

You're celibate. Control yourself.

Under the table, Lex pinched his thigh until the image of her spread across his bed and open to his every desire disappeared. But, damn, it was hard. *He* was hard.

"I think you're trying to play me." Noelle blew across the surface of her hot tea, her lips pursed and her eyes perceptive. "But my sister threw me to the lions today so I might as well play with one. Right?"

Lex wondered again why Margot thought her sister needed a fake lover to heal an old wound that he sensed was on its way to being mended already. This woman was strong. And she was breaking down every one of his defenses.

"I wouldn't call myself a lion," Lex managed with a smile. "Just a friendly pussycat."

Noelle made a disbelieving noise. "Have some more tea," she said. "It's getting cold."

They finished her pot of tea and his glass of taro smoothie, sharing their different experiences of the tea shop—when they'd first discovered it, who brought them, their favorite thing to eat or drink there. At first, Lex asked these questions to distract himself from how breathtaking she was, how knee-weakeningly sexy. Then it was because he really wanted to know about her and was pleased that, although Margot was the one who told him about the tea shop, he liked it nearly as much as Noelle seemed to, having visited it twice before the day Margot had arranged for them to meet.

Because he was Jamaican, tea was part of his everyday life. He drank a hot cup every morning and sometimes before bed. The different varieties at the shop exposed him to new flavors he'd never tried before.

He'd already bought a few ounces of different teas to drink at home.

"If you're ever curious enough to try a few select tea blends," he told Noelle while smiling around the last small bite of the sandwich, "you should come over to my kitchen. I have some tea from here that you might like. In case you're ever fiending for a cup when they're closed."

Noelle almost grinned, Lex could tell. "I'll keep that in mind," she said.

"Please do. It's a very sincere invitation." Lex winked at her, feeling a bit silly. But her brief look of amusement made it worth it. Noelle made him want to say and do the most ridiculous things just to see that sparkle in her eyes.

He drained the last of his tea and was about to suggest they get another pot, this time something that he recommended, when his phone vibrated in his pocket. Frowning, he excused himself to answer it.

It was Kingsley. "Hey, what's up?"

"Not much." His brother sounded distracted. "Have you talked with Alice about the new project she's working on?"

"No. Why?"

"I don't think it's legit. She may be getting taken for a ride on this. Can you take a look at it? We're at her apartment. There's some computer-coding stuff I don't get. And I don't think she understands it either. It could come back to bite her in the ass."

Dammit. Not today. "No problem," Lex said. "I'll come over there now."

"Okay. I'll see you soon."

Lex hung up the phone with a look of apology. "I

have to head out." He was more than reluctant to go, but his family needed him.

"If I didn't know better, I'd say folks are allergic to my presence today." Noelle's tone was wry.

"Only if they're allergic to beautiful and charming women." Lex pulled out his wallet and a ten-dollar bill to leave for the tip. After a moment's hesitation, more for show than anything, he also took out a business card and scribbled his number and name on the back of it. "I would love to see you again."

Noelle slid the card into her purse. "We'll see what happens." She stood up. "At least your call waited until we finished our food."

"My family is nothing if not courteous," he said. Or some of them were.

Noelle stood up and walked with Lex toward the front door. He held it open for her to go first.

In the parking lot, he walked her to her car, hyperaware of her thoughtful silence. Something suddenly occurred to him. Something Margot may not have known.

"Are you seeing someone?" he asked. The thought of it made him nearly sick, but it made sense to ask. "Because if you are, I'll back off. I don't want to break up anyone's happy home."

She touched the side of her neck, skated long fingers up behind her ear, lightly touching the shell-like curve like she was listening for something. It was the same gesture her sister often made, but, on Noelle, it made the breath stutter in Lex's chest. He imagined her touching him like that, her fingers light down his chest like a promise. "I'm not seeing anyone," she said and gave him permission to breathe again. "I'm not really in that place right now. Or at least I wasn't until very recently."

Despite the circumstances, foolish hope sputtered to life in his chest. Just maybe she would allow herself to want him and to say yes to whatever was brewing between them. He liked Noelle very much and wanted to see her again, separate from anything Margot wanted him to do.

His phone vibrated again, probably Kingsley telling him to hurry it up. He pulled it out of his pocket and glanced at his brother's number.

"I have to go," he said, his finger hovering over the screen. "But call me. I'll have tea and anything else you need." He felt another glow of triumph at the almost smile on her face. "See you soon. Yes?"

She nodded and waved him away. "Go answer your call."

Lex turned away, grabbing the call before it got sent to voice mail. "I'm on the way," he said.

"Are you on a date?" Kingsley asked.

"Why are you asking?" Lex was fully prepared for his brother to make fun of him about his short-lived celibacy, but that didn't come.

"Don't worry about the meeting. Wolfe is looking into it right now. He's at home on his laptop right now. If there's anything we can't take care of, I'll call you back. But things should be cool."

Lex slowed his footsteps on the way to his car. "Are you sure?"

"Yeah. We can handle this one. Go back to the unlucky girl. Hope she knows you're not giving anything up."

"Thanks for the reminder."

"Anytime."

Lex was already turning to Noelle when his brother hung up, his heart beating fast with possibility. Across the parking lot, she climbed into her car. He tucked his phone away and waved to her, walked quickly (*not* ran) to get her attention before she drove away. He wanted more of her.

It was a fault of his, he knew, this endless hunger for pleasure, grabbing more and more of whatever felt good since he never knew when it would end. He wanted so much more but didn't want to scare Noelle away. He was a stranger who basically bogarted his way into her private tea party. And even though their attraction was mutual, she was cautious of him. Rightly so.

Still, nothing ventured and all that.

Lex called out her name as he approached her car, and she looked up from her cell phone, a smile twitching across her face.

"I'm unexpectedly free for the rest of the day," he said, bracing his hands on the roof of the car. "Do you want to do this some more?"

Her gaze was a naked flame, alternately hot then simmering, moving over his face, searching. "Yeah, why not?" she said at last, her voice a slow and thoughtful hum. "Get in."

He got into her car without a second thought, although, right after issuing the invitation, Noelle immediately looked ready to take it back. Lex flashed her a smile and sank into the cloth seat that smelled vaguely of coconuts.

After he made himself comfortable, reclining the seat as far back as it could go and stretching out his legs, he let down the automatic window and waited for her to start the car. He didn't care where they were going. Teatime was over—that much was clear. The car started up and a slow, bass-heavy song began to play. The Weeknd. Lex felt her taking peeks at him, but he continued to look forward, enjoying the feel of the breeze through the window, the sunlight on his face.

"So, if it's not too private, what were your plans for the day?" she asked.

Kiss every part of you until you're a whimpering mess under my mouth, and then take you hard and rough until we're both hoarse from shouting. He licked his lips and rolled his head on the headrest to look outside. *Or just, you know, stay celibate.* "No plans," Lex said instead. "I had a meeting this morning and after that, nothing in stone. I like to keep my weekends flexible."

Beside him, she kept both hands on the steering wheel at ten and two, sitting upright in the seat, her back straight. Despite her posture, though, she actually seemed comfortable, turning her eyes away from the road to look at him every so often while the car rolled smoothly toward wherever they were going.

She smelled like the tea shop, hints of the sweetness of taro in the flutter of her shirt from the car's breeze, the faintest traces of green tea caught in her hair. Lex allowed himself the brief fantasy of reaching up to tangle his fingers in her hair, pulling her down to feel her soft mouth on his, the hot dance of her tongue.

He blamed The Weeknd's baby-making music.

"You mind if I change the station?" he asked.

"Not at all. Go for it."

He played with the knobs of the sound system until

he found a reggae station playing grooves from the seventies. Smooth and mellow. Nothing distracting. He hummed along to the music. Felt the corners of his own mouth lift when Noelle smiled.

Minutes later, they arrived in what looked like North Beach and pulled onto a side street. At four o'clock on a Saturday, in the middle of a Miami autumn, the sidewalk was far from crowded. More locals than tourists. The whisper of the beach from across the street, food trucks parked next to the sidewalks pouring out delicious, meaty smells.

Lex sat up in the car. "What's the party for?"

"Do we ever need a reason to party?"

"Nope."

When she stopped the car, he climbed out and stretched. Lex pretended not to notice Noelle watching his shirt ride up to expose his stomach and the blue stripe of his underwear. He'd always been aware of his body, of its effect on women back when he'd been muscular and pumped from his five-days-a-week gym regimen. These days, he was more into doing laps in the pool instead of lifting weights and it showed in his wider shoulders and less dense torso. No one ever complained though. He twitched his shirt a little higher before settling it back around his hips.

"Nice." His jaw cracked open with a yawn. "I wish I was hungry enough to get something from over here." It smelled damn good.

"We can grab something after my class."

Class? He tilted his chin. An obvious question.

"I have a dance class here." Her eyes skipped away from him when she said it, like she was embarrassed and trying not to be. "It starts around six and goes until seven thirty. We can get a bite to eat after."

"Hmm. I like how you think." He leaned close, keeping his voice low and secretive. "I love stuff like this. Outdoor food. When I was a kid, I could never get enough of the state fair."

Shaking her head, she locked the car door and shouldered her purse. "Come." He could see her smile peeking out at the seams.

Lex fell into step beside her as she took off across the sidewalk toward the sand. "What about you? What's your stance on food trucks? Sensational or unsanitary?"

Noelle was trying too hard not to laugh. He could tell by the faint crease on her forehead, the dip in her cheek betraying that she was biting the inside of her mouth. Sweet thing.

"This is serious," Lex said. He was on the hunt to tease more out of her. Her humor, her love of pleasure hovered just beneath her neutral looks, waiting to be scratched to the surface. "Our entire relationship from this point on depends on your answer to that question." He tilted his eyebrow at her.

"Why are you so silly?"

"Why are you avoiding the question?"

She shook her head and pushed past him, her Converse sneakers sinking into the sand. "Food trucks are all right," she tossed over her shoulder.

Her bottom, ripe and entrancing, shifted under the jeans and the shapeless T-shirt draped attractively over her hips. Lex stopped staring long enough to jog after her. He easily caught up in a few strides of his long legs. "I think you're being coy," he said. "You're hiding a secret love from me. I guess we'll find out later."

"Maybe we will," she said.

Laughter sizzled at the back of his throat. "Definitely a tease," he said.

They walked across the sand together, aimless and slow, his sandals sifting through sand with every step. The granules were warm against his toes, the sun a burning kiss along his cheek and throat, through his thin T-shirt. With a look at the horizon, Lex realized he and Noelle had already been together for at least three hours. It still felt easy and very, very good. So good that it all felt like a risk. Margot. His celibacy. The things he wanted to share with Noelle despite the very tricky situation he'd put himself in.

"Are you a risk taker, Noelle?" he asked. The waves rippled with foam along the sand's edge.

"Uh…" She blinked, surprise at the question all over her pretty face. "Strange. I was actually just thinking about risk."

Interesting. He resisted the urge to make their conversation a more serious one and find out exactly what she was thinking if it was about him.

"Were you thinking you might—" the corner of Lex's mouth ticked up "—take a chance on me?"

Noelle breathed out an almost sigh, her eyes like black diamonds in the sun. Then she shook her head. "You can probably tell." She gestured to herself, but he didn't know what he was supposed to assume from her gorgeous body and soft-looking mouth. "Everything's conservative about me, except the way I vote."

"I can guess a lot of things by looking at you," he said. "Conservative is not one that comes immediately to mind." He licked the corner of his mouth and his eyes swept her from head to toe. "Not at all."

Noelle hid her reaction by bending to pull off her shoes and socks, but not before he saw the flare of heat in her eyes, the touch of color in her cheeks. He let her ignore his blatant innuendo, shrugged off the effect of his own words on himself.

"Looking at me, people tend to make assumptions," he said. "About the things I like, the way I dress. The music I listen to. But I think they'd be wrong about most things."

"You mean you actually are *not* comfortable in your own skin and do *not* love to seduce strange women to your place for tea?"

He laughed, watching the effect the sound of it had on her, the subtle opening of her body, arms falling over her stomach. "Well, that much is true." He'd been on the verge of telling her about his past, how he once did things just for the sake of doing them and had been trying to be a better man for nearly eight years now. But he said none of that.

"Risk can be sweet," he said instead, referring back to his earlier comment. "Even in something as small as being the opposite of what people expect to find under your conservative layers."

"That's not me," Noelle said, and a shadow floated across her features, pulling her mouth tight.

The sight of that twisted an answering unhappiness in Lex's belly. "No one is saying you should jump out of a plane without a parachute," he said. "It can be simple things." The waves snaked up to the sand, grabbing at his sandals, and Noelle danced back from the water, keeping her black tennis shoes dry. That gave him an idea.

Lex pulled out his wallet and threw it at her. She easily caught it and frowned at him. "What—?"

He started walking backward into the shifting water.

"Are you serious right now?" Her hands flexed around the wallet, eyes wide in disbelief.

He kept walking backward into the water, feeling the sun on his face, the intoxication of having her complete attention. "Risks, right?" He cocked his head at her and smiled in invitation. "You want to come in with me?"

"No, thanks." She looked alarmed, watching the water rise above his knees, to his thighs. Noelle gestured to him. "Come over here. You don't have to do anything like this." She was trying to be calm, maybe even nonchalant, but she danced close to the waves and then away, trying to get him to return to the dry sand. "Get your ass back here. You'll ruin your clothes."

But Lex walked back farther until the waves and the sand pulled him down and he fell into the warm water, laughing. God! It felt good, the salt in his mouth, the water heavy in his clothes and against his skin. It had been a while since he'd been to the beach and gotten into the water. He floated and watched her on the shore, her hands gripping his wallet against her chest.

"You're nuts," she shouted to him over the sound of the waves.

But she looked lonely there on the sand, even with the other people on the beach watching him and her, some with their cell phone cameras pointed at him. The water would feel even better if she was in the water with him to share its warmth. Lex stood up and waded his way back to her, the water dragging at his clothes, dripping from him with every step.

"Risk doesn't have to be anything big," he said with a laugh. On relatively stable sand, he went to her, tapped a wet finger on her nose. "You get wet and then you get dry. Simple."

She actually giggled this time, eyes sparkling at him as the wind played in her hair. "What about your phone, smart-ass?"

Lex pulled his iPhone from his pocket, safe in its waterproof case. "I may step on the edge every once in a while, but I'm not crazy."

Noelle laughed then, and he didn't know which of them was more shocked. The musical sound of it rang out over the waves and pulled him under her spell just a little bit more.

Chapter 6

Lex came out of the water like a sea god. Surprising muscles rippling under his wet T-shirt, the jeans clinging to solid thighs she could easily imagine holding on to while he fisted a hand in her hair. Noelle bit her lip, feeling her heart race with the unexpected arousal even as she laughed at his ridiculousness.

She backed away from him as he came closer, not wanting to get wet. "Was all that risk worth your wet clothes?"

"Absolutely." He smiled, a spread of his full mouth, white teeth, light brown eyes crinkling at the corners. And there was something about the way he looked at her through water-spiked lashes that made her think of marathon sex, both of them dripping sweat and sliding against each other toward satisfaction.

Not where she needed her mind to be right now.

"Lucky for you, there's a store around here where you can grab something to replace all that." She dipped her head toward his clothes and dragged her gaze, greedy and thorough, over every wet inch of him presented to her.

"Lucky me," Lex murmured.

Noelle took him to the T.J. Maxx nearby, where he bought a nearly identical outfit—jeans, undershirt, button-down shirt—and then he tossed the bag with his wet clothes into her trunk.

"Problem solved," he said as they walked from her car toward the studio where she had her scheduled dance class.

"Thanks to me," she said.

"Credit absolutely where credit is due."

Her class was a few blocks from the beach in a four-story building with wide windows and questionable air circulation.

"I don't want you to be bored," Noelle said. "Are you sure you want to come up here with me?"

She realized a moment later that she was asking the question too late. They'd already left his car at the tea shop and spent nearly two hours together after their drive to North Beach. But she recognized the anxiety for what it was. This was something she did for herself and that no one else in her life knew about. Not Margot, not the girls she hung out with most weekends, not even her therapist. It was her own private therapy to get her body moving, to get her mind focused on something besides her shortcomings.

"I'm good," Lex said, walking and easy by her side. "If I'm bored, I'll let you know."

In the class, most of the students were already there.

Nearly a dozen of them, Noelle included, already in their dance clothes. The girls wore yoga pants and tight shirts while the guys wore sweats or basketball shorts, most already gathered in their established cliques. The two girls Noelle usually talked with, Ruby and Malia, sat on the floor doing stretches and chatting with the instructor, Milton.

"Is this weird?" Noelle suddenly felt like she was messing up by bringing Lex to the class. She looked at her two friends, who spotted her and waved, and then she narrowed her eyes at Lex. "I think this is weird."

"What?" He looked so curious, so amused at everything around him. Like nothing could faze him.

"I'm dragging a stranger to what's basically my therapy group." Then she flushed, realizing what she had just said. *Damn.* "I'm going to change." She ran off and left him to fend for himself.

When she came back from stashing her bag and changing in the locker room, he was sitting on the long bench at the front of the room talking to Milton. Noelle was torn between sitting with her friends and going to rescue Lex from Milton, who was an aggressive flirt.

"Hey, girl!"

Ruby, short with thick hips and the tiniest waist Noelle had ever seen on a human, stood up to hug Noelle. "Who is that hot piece of action you brought with you?" She pursed her naturally red lips, her black eyes narrowed with naked curiosity.

"Yeah." Malia craned her head in the most unsubtle way possible. She was the very opposite of Ruby, tall and willowy, an albino beauty with freckles scattered across her nose. "Milton is already trying to get some of that."

But Ruby shook her head. "I think, for once, Milton is just having a conversation with him, not trying to take him home or anything."

Sure enough, the men were simply...talking. Lex was laughing about something Milton was saying while their dance instructor made wild gestures like he was trying to ride an extra-tall, invisible tree. A few of their classmates migrated toward the two men.

"I'll go check it out. I don't want him to be uncomfortable," Noelle said.

She made to step away, but Ruby grabbed her arm. "I need the 411 before you run off. Anyway, I think your lover boy is fine. He doesn't look like the kind of guy whose masculinity is threatened by conversation with a gay man." And Milton was very obviously gay.

Across the room, Lex was obviously enjoying himself, laughing with Milton and a few of the other guys. Noelle allowed Ruby to pull her down on the floor between her and Malia. She hadn't known the girls very long, only for the five weeks she'd been in the class. But she had clicked with them both, although more so with Ruby. They were generous and funny women who didn't demand anything more than her company and conversation. For the short time they had been friends, she felt closer to them than to most other people in her life.

"There's no big story to tell," Noelle said. "I met him today at the tea shop and we've just been hanging out since then."

"That's what you pick up from the tea shop?" Malia looked over her shoulder again, her pale eyes sparkling. "Maybe I should start drinking some of that boba mess too."

"So you're on a date?" Ruby's little teeth were bared in a disconcerting grin. She looked hungry for information. It was scary and funny at the same time.

"Not a date." Noelle tilted a look over her shoulder at Lex, drinking in his arresting beauty. "But I like him."

"That means you can't touch, Malia." Ruby wagged a threatening finger at their friend.

"As if I'd poach a man another girl brought around."

Ruby made a rude noise but didn't say anything else about that. "Whatever you're doing to keep him interested, keep it up," she said. "That man is yummy."

Malia bumped Noelle's shoulder. "Introduce us."

When they walked up to Lex and Milton, Noelle realized that the men were speaking a foreign language. When he noticed her, Lex grinned and switched back to English she could understand.

"Noelle. Milton here is from Jamaica too, the same parish where my people are from."

Milton followed suit and started speaking in English again. "I've met a few people from all over the island, but not many of them are from Annotto Bay. He's practically my brother." The two men looked nothing alike though. Milton's features were narrow and more European, wrapped in silt-dark skin, while Lex was simply…Lex. Pale and potent, what she imagined a Yoruba deity of sexuality would look like in the world.

On the bench next to Milton, Lex nodded, a smile playing around his mobile mouth. "True. My grandparents moved from there when they were young, but the family goes back often. Milton and I used to climb the same trees and go to the same beach."

"A lot happened while I was changing my clothes," Noelle said.

"A lot happened today," Lex said by way of agreement. "All good things. And I'm hoping for more."

Noelle felt her friends' eyes on her, saw Milton's knowing smile. "Nice," Milton said. "We were all blessed today."

A soft chime sounded from the watch on Milton's wrist and suddenly he was all business. "Time for us to start class, everybody." He clapped his hands, a sharp and loud sound in the room. He gave Lex an apologetic smile, but Lex made a smooth motion of his shoulders, a shrug of understanding.

The other students, eleven in all, streamed from their separate corners of the room and gathered in front of Milton.

He clapped his hands again. "Everyone, we'll be learning the second part of the routine I introduced last class. As usual, watch me first and then we'll practice the separate parts of the routine together."

Lex slipped away to a far wall of the large classroom and sat on one of the three stools there. It took more effort than she thought it would, but Noelle eventually blocked out his presence to fall into the rhythm and movements of the class. More than once during the session, though, she found her attention wandering to Lex, the spread of his legs, the way he braced his forearms on his thighs to dangle his hands between them. Whenever she looked at him, he was already watching her.

When they finally took a break, Noelle was sweating even more than usual, damp and trembling everywhere fabric touched her skin.

While the rest of the class limped off to recover, Milton went up to change the music on the iPod. "What do you think?" Noelle heard him ask Lex, who seemed criminally dry while everyone else dripped with sweat and panted like dogs on hot pavement.

"Nice work," Lex said, flicking a warm look toward Noelle that she felt all the way to her toes. "I've seen a few people break it down in the club like this, but it's nice to see the work that goes into it."

"The club?" Milton looked insulted.

"A practical application of a skill set," Lex reassured him. "Not everyone will get the chance to audition for the next *Bring It On*."

Behind him, Ruby mouthed "*Bring It On*?" Malia choked on her laughter.

"His pop culture references are a little dated," Noelle said under her breath.

"No kidding," Malia muttered. "And why would he even know about *Bring It On*? Are you sure he's straight?"

"He's straight enough," Noelle said.

This time, Malia didn't even try to hide her laughter. Milton ignored them all, all except for Lex anyway.

"Since you know about *Bring It On*, you want to come dance with us?"

Lex laughed and shook his head. "Nope. The only kind of dancing I do is in front of the mirror."

Milton raised a naughty eyebrow. "Now that I'd pay to see."

"Me too," Ruby chimed in.

Noelle rolled her eyes. "You all are a bunch of perverts."

Malia lightly pinched her side and leaned close. "As if you wouldn't."

Although she would never admit it to a soul, the thought of Lex dancing in front of the mirror, his hips bucking in the tight, blue briefs she'd briefly glimpsed earlier, haunted Noelle for the rest of the class. It was a miracle she didn't trip over her feet.

At the end of the class, Noelle was dripping with sweat. She groped for her towel as she sank down on the bench next to Ruby and Malia.

"Oh my God. Why did I think this was a good idea?" Her heart was pounding hard in her chest and she felt like she had only got half the routine right.

"Because it's fun?" Malia wiped her face with her own towel and dropped her head back against the wall.

"Painful fun." Ruby giggled.

"You want to come with us for dinner?"

Noelle dragged the towel from her face when she heard Milton ask the question not to her but to Lex, who stood nearby with a brochure for the class in his hand.

"Ooh, he's trying to take your man." Malia was not at all subtle with her so-called whisper.

"He's not my man," Noelle said. But she waited for Lex's response. Already, he didn't seem to care that Milton was gay and seemed completely flexible about where his evening went.

"Another time," Lex said. "Noelle and I have plans. But we should exchange numbers. I could always use another friend in Miami."

Malia made a noise next to Noelle as if she had just got confirmation about something.

Ruby gave Malia a laughing look. "It is possible for a gay man and a straight man to be friends without them ending up naked wrestling, you know." She stuffed her towel into her gym bag.

"Anything is possible. But if they do end up naked wrestling, I want to watch."

"Malia!" Noelle stared at her friend but couldn't help laughing.

"Damn, Malia!" Ruby wore a serious face for all of five seconds before laughing too. "That's *not* something you say to a girl trying to get some straight-man sausage. Anyway, Noelle's not looking for a sandwich, just a little old-fashioned man meat pie, straight up." She pointed her index finger at the ceiling.

"Now you're just making me hungry." Noelle playfully shoved at Ruby and then threw her towel over her shoulder. "I'm going to wash up." She looked up and caught Lex's eye, saw his upraised brow, which she instinctively knew meant he had something to say to her. "Excuse me." She went over to join him just as Milton walked away.

"Hey, you were great out there." His voice was a low and pleasant hum, sliding over her sweat-damp skin like a caress.

A serpentine shiver worked its slow way through her body, waking up every nerve that hadn't already been hyperaware of him. "Thanks," she said. "I like to dance and…this place is good for me." Although he hadn't brought it up, she stressed again the therapeutic nature of the class.

"Yeah. I can see that. We all need to do things for ourselves that feel good." His eyes moved over her, lingering on her thighs and the cradle of her hips that were all the more visible in her thin sweats. Then he smiled, a hungry tiger abruptly caged. "You ready to head out or do you want to have dinner with your friends?"

"You and I already have plans." She echoed his earlier words to let him know she'd heard him. "Just give me a few minutes to grab a quick shower and change."

But Lex leaned close, his height making the action more intimate than it would have been with a taller man. His breath hovered at her throat and she felt herself quivering with awareness of him.

"You smell fine to me," he said. "Like a good night's work. Nothing to be ashamed of."

Noelle heartily disagreed with him. The sweat had poured hard from her, stinging her eyes, slicking her armpits and her back. He, on the other hand, was dry as a bone and looked as cool (and lickable) as ice cream.

"I'm not ashamed," she muttered while surreptitiously trying to sniff herself.

"Good. Put your street shoes back on and we can leave. The food trucks won't be there forever."

Seriously? Noelle bit her lip to stifle her laughter. "You just want me to leave here stinking so you can put some food in your belly!" He really *did* love to eat.

"You smell like something I'd like to eat," he said with a playful growl. "It's only fair we get something nutritionally sound in my stomach before I make you an indecent proposal."

Heat rushed under Noelle's skin and she nearly embarrassed herself with a full-on moan. "I'm not really sure how to take that," she said once she could talk again.

"Take it any way you like, as long as we get some food in here." He patted his belly with a grin.

She snorted a laugh but shook her head. "I absolutely *have* to shower. I'll make it a quick one though."

Lex looked disappointed but didn't try again to talk her out of it. "I'm timing you." He made a show of looking at his naked wrist, like a watch was there ticking away the minutes.

When Noelle told Malia and Ruby she was leaving with Lex after a quick shower, Malia laughed at her. "I thought you were just going to leave here without even taking a ho bath." The three women walked to the locker room together.

"That would be *hot*," Ruby said with a grin. "Leave here sweaty and get even sweatier with him later on. But cleaning up to get dirty can be fun too."

Noelle didn't bother to correct her. Ruby was a happy proponent of doing whatever you feel, whenever you feel it. For her, it didn't matter that Noelle had just met Lex. Ruby, after surviving a brain tumor, was all about carpe diem. Sex was fun. Life was for living. Tomorrow may never come.

After they had showered, she passed Noelle a six-pack of condoms. "Here, honey. In case you weren't prepared." But Noelle, blushing so hard it felt like her face was on fire, drew the line at that. "I'm good," she said. "I don't think I'll need these today."

"You never know." Ruby dropped the condoms in Noelle's bag anyway and clicked her own purse shut. "Joy comes at unexpected times." She winked and started pulling her gym bag from her locker. "Have fun and tell us all about it next time we see you."

"Whatever you do, have fun." Malia was already packed and waiting for the usually slow Ruby to finish getting her things together. "And call us if you need anything."

"Yes, honey. Call if you need anything at all." Ruby pressed a kiss to Noelle's cheek and Noelle clung to her, feeling blessed at the kindness and unconditional support these women showed her. Ruby and Malia had their own problems—they all did—but the women were also looking for a healthy escape from different parts of their lives, and they found that in each other.

"I will," Noelle said. "See you in a couple of days."

"Later, babe." After a quick swat at Noelle's behind, Ruby grabbed her bag to finish packing up. "And have fun tonight. No regrets." Her dirty laugh said exactly what kind of fun she expected Noelle to have.

After she left the locker room and said her good-byes to Milton, Noelle found Lex at the bench just putting his phone away. Whatever conversation he'd just finished had left little frown lines in his forehead.

"Everything okay?" she asked him.

He shrugged. "Okay enough." His gaze took a quick and appreciative journey up and then down her body. She wore a high-waisted, floral jumpsuit she'd tucked into her bag at the last minute before leaving the house, paired with her Converse shoes. He gestured at her gym bag. "You need help with that?"

She shook her head at his misplaced chivalry. "No, it's not heavy. Besides, you didn't help me with it when I brought it in."

He chuckled, a soft and intimate sound. "True."

Outside, the sun was long gone. Noelle drew in a deep breath of the evening air that had just a touch of coolness to it. Fall in Miami.

"Thanks for coming with me to my dance class. I know it was random."

"It was fun. I enjoyed watching you dance. You do it well."

She warmed at the compliment, although, compared to the others in the class, she was as graceful as a new-born foal. "Thanks. It's something I enjoy, although I wasn't sure I would."

"But you signed up for it anyway?"

"Yeah. I…" She snagged her lower lip between her teeth, second-guessing what she was about to say. In her head, the words didn't sound too damning. "I come here twice a week and dance to Beyoncé and Pitbull. It feels good. Before I signed up for this, I'd go clubbing sometimes and dance by myself." Noelle thought about the same booty-bouncing dance she'd been doing since she was a teen. "But one day I was leaving an appointment near here—" he didn't need to know it was with her therapist "—and saw the sign for dance lessons. I went in on a whim and it's been one of the best decisions I've made in a long time."

"I can see why. You were glowing in there. We should all do something nice for ourselves every once in a while." A secret smile curved Lex's mouth and, with the light from the street lamps gilding his face as they walked back to the car, he looked even more beautiful. Noelle swore she'd never seen a prettier man in real life.

"What nice things do you do for yourself?" she asked just for an excuse to stare at him.

"Just today I asked a beautiful woman to have tea with me." His teeth flashed in the golden street light.

Like he must have intended, she nearly laughed. "Why does everything you say sound like a cheesy pickup line?"

"Really? I need to work on that. You're the first one to say I'm cheesy. Charm is kinda my thing."

Laughter tickled her throat again, but she swallowed it. "Your *thing*?"

"Yeah. Or maybe it *was*, past tense. Apparently, I need to up my charm game."

At her car, she tossed her gym bag in the trunk and tucked a slim wallet into the zippered pocket of her jumpsuit. "Ready?"

"Born ready."

This time, she did laugh. At the food trucks, the area was even more crowded. There were lights on the trucks to illuminate the chefs serving food and the long lines at most of them. The street was busier with people sitting on the sidewalk eating their food or walking toward the beach. Conversation flavored the air, along with the smell of roasted meats, corn dog batter and the bite of lemons from a nearby lemonade-and-natural-juice truck.

Noelle drew in a deep lungful of the tempting flavors and looked up and then down the block. "I don't even know where to start."

Beside her, Lex cracked his knuckles like he was getting ready for battle. "It's always good to start at the beginning," he said.

He pointed to the very first truck in the lineup, which also happened to have a giant corn dog painted on the side. The batter on the sign looked both crisp and doughy, and the sign itself advertised beef and turkey, as well as jalapeno, corn dogs.

"Lead on," she said with a wave of her hand.

After stopping at every truck, they agreed on a turkey-jalapeno corn dog, a spiced-apple-and-Havarti grilled cheese sandwich and funnel cake to share, and then they got a large lemonade and sat down on a just-vacated bench to eat. Lex put the food between them, along with a giant stack of napkins.

"I'm a messy eater," he said when she glanced at the napkins without saying a word.

And although he didn't mean it in the way Noelle hoped he meant it, she still clenched her thighs tight and swallowed hard. "Napkins are good for that," she said, deliberately not looking at him.

But when he chuckled, a low and rumbling sound too dirty to be innocent, she thought maybe he did know what she was thinking. She cleared her throat and plucked at the funnel cake until powdered sugar clung to her fingers.

"I think this whole food-truck revolution is kind of amazing," she said to distract them both from the heat wavering between them. "I only go to state fairs and theme parks for the food." Noelle made the confession without looking up from the funnel cake she was slowly tearing apart and feeding herself, tiny piece by tiny piece. "This way, I can skip the rides and everything else that would ruin a good time and just enjoy the real reason for me leaving my house."

She expected him to make some remark about her weight or the grease from fair food. Instead, Lex just grinned and tore into the grilled cheese sandwich between them, catching a slice of the softened apple that threatened to fall from the corner of his mouth. "That's the only reason I go on dates," he said, his cheeks puffed with the savory-sweet mixture of multigrain bread, apples and cheese. "For the food."

She choked on her laughter and an ill-timed sip of her lemonade, had to press a hand to her chest through a coughing fit. "I don't believe you! How can you have a body like that and love food like you say?"

"Ah…" Lex batted his eyelashes at her, a smile curving shallow lines at the corners of his mouth. "You think I'm pretty."

"Pretty damn conceited."

But she didn't think he was fooled by her stumbling reply. It had to be obvious how she felt. Since they had met in the tea shop, she'd been staring at him like he was her next meal. His own fault, really, since no man should be this appealing in real life. His sense of humor was ridiculous. *He* was ridiculous. But she loved to hear him laugh and even his attempts at flattery were sweet, transparent and utterly charming, though she'd never tell him that.

Noelle held up the last of the funnel cake. "You want this?"

"I do, but I'm gentleman enough to let you have it." He reached for the corn dog. "I'll make do with this." He waggled the deep-fried dough studded with jalapeno slices in front of her face before chomping down on a quarter of the dog in one bite. His expression when the food hit his taste buds was, if she had to describe it, pure ecstasy. She shifted in her seat and then reached for the lemonade to wet her suddenly dry throat.

"That's good…" he said once he swallowed the ridiculously large bite.

"It sure looked like it." She reached for the corn dog. "My turn now."

She was sure she didn't imagine his hesitation. When she had the dog in her hand, she held it close to her body in case he wanted to reach over and try to take it from her. "Are you an only child?"

"Far from it." He stuck the lemonade straw in his mouth. "One of thirteen."

"Your parents Catholic?"

"Just horny, I think."

Does it run in the family? But Noelle kept that question to herself, stuffing the corn dog into her mouth instead of saying another word. But *oh*...

"It's good as hell, right?" He looked smug, like he'd been the one to make the damn corn dog.

But it was good. Really, *really* good.

"Mmm. Very."

Noelle chewed, unable to help the smile of utter pleasure that took over her face. She really loved food. Too much, some people said. But she didn't feel she had a problem.

When she looked up from the now empty corn dog stick, she drew a swift breath. Lex's eyes were on her and no longer smiling but watching with an unmistakable hunger.

"I'm sure you know how sexy you are." His voice was a low and rough growl. "But *damn* I want to take you to bed so bad it hurts." He shifted against the hard bench and then jerked his head away. After a long moment, he breathed out, loud and fast. Then he turned to her with a forced smile. "Forget I said that."

As if she could. Noelle swallowed the sudden moisture in her mouth. The last bite of the corn dog had slid across her tongue with the sweetness of honey mated with the pepper's spice. A delicious commingling of flavors that left her lips burning and sticky. She was still hungry. But not for food.

Slow down. Don't get caught up. Remember what happened with Eric.

But it didn't matter. Her body, usually dormant until her heart was involved, tingled all over from one look Lex turned her way. A slick heat moved between her

thighs. Her heartbeat sped up. She bit her lip and wondered, not for the first time that night, what the hell was
wrong with her. Why did a stranger, *this* stranger, do
it for her when Eric had to damn near do circus tricks
to make her lose breath? Then her thoughts stuttered
to a halt.

Lex had leaned close to her, his eyes resting on
her lips. Her own eyes fluttered shut in anticipation
of his kiss, of his mouth that had been distracting her
all night with its plump sheen and the gleam of teeth
beyond, which made her imagine herself a fine bit of
pastry begging for him to sink himself into. She held
her breath, waited. Then she jumped at the feel of his
thumb at the side of her mouth. A brush of a slightly
callused finger against her soft flesh.

"You had a crumb," he said, his voice low and rough.

She flushed and jerked her eyes open.

Idiot.

But his body remained inclined toward her on the
bench and there was nothing funny in the way he
looked at her. Noelle had never been a bold girl. She'd
wanted men before but often waited until they made
the move. But she felt an almost savage urge to climb
into Lex's lap and kiss him. The urge was so strong
that she had to clench her hands in her lap and back
away from him.

"Thanks," she said.

"No problem."

Around them, it had grown dark, the air filled with
the sounds of strangers enjoying the night and the scent
of roasting meat and green peppers from the nearest
food truck. But during that moment while she waited
for Lex to kiss her, everything had disappeared. Smells.

Sounds. Even the sensation of the ocean breeze on her skin became muted. It was just her and Lex and the possibility of their bodies coming together.

A couple walked past them, sharing a basket of fries. "Do you want to stay for the fireworks?" the taller woman asked as they wandered past and toward the beach. Noelle didn't hear the other woman's reply. She turned to Lex. "Fireworks?"

"Yes," he said.

When they finished eating, Lex picked up the debris of their meal and took it to the trash. The slow dip of his hips in the tight jeans, a mouthwatering swagger, was the sexiest thing she'd seen in a long time. She stared at the firm rise of his butt under the denim and then looked away before he could turn around and catch her.

"We can use my shirt as a blanket," he said, walking back from the nearby trash can.

She didn't protest.

On the beach, they found a spot among the scattering of couples, friends and families spread out on colorful blankets. As promised, Lex took off his button-down shirt and spread it over the sand for her. After she sat on the makeshift blanket, he settled himself next to her with a sigh. Noelle drew in a breath and smelled only him, the salt that had settled into his skin from his earlier swim in the ocean, the faint department-store scent of his new clothes, a hint of the lemonade on his breath.

The white undershirt stretched over his chest and left his bare and sculpted arms under the clear night sky. He wasn't a six-pack model, but his body was lean and firm, subtle with muscle and gleaming skin. Idly, she wondered what kind of lotion he used to keep his skin so soft and supple-looking even after an unplanned dip in the ocean. Anything to stop her mind from going to sensual places with the sight of so much beautiful bare skin. The heat from his body both soothed and scalded her. She wanted to curl up in his lap. She wanted to kiss him and drag him down into the sand with her.

All righty then.

The first explosion of fireworks lit up the sky in a shower of bright yellow and green. A low sound of pleasure came from Lex as he tilted his head to look up at the sky. He leaned so far that his back was nearly parallel to the ground. She touched his shoulder, opened her mouth to invite him to lay his head in her lap so he wouldn't strain his neck.

Don't.

He looked at her when she touched him, but she shook her head. "Nothing."

But his neck must have hurt because he turned his head away only to lie down in the sand, sinking his beautiful body down into the pale bed of granules, one knee raised up, the other stretched out. The light from the fireworks above burst over his skin in bright whites, electric blues and fiery reds. Lex folded his arms behind his head, smiling, eyes following the flow of colors above. But, for Noelle, it was better, more beautiful, to watch the explosion of color in the joy on his face.

He looked at her, and his smile was inviting and warm, and she felt it all through her. Lex nudged her foot with his own and turned back to the sky, still smiling. His beauty squeezed her throat tight. So tight that, for a moment, she couldn't breathe.

Noelle turned away from him and squeezed her eyes

shut. This was something she didn't need, this attraction. But it felt so precious, so warm, that she squeezed her thighs together and sighed. Quietly. Keeping it to herself just for a few minutes more.

"I can never decide which I like better," Lex said, apropos of nothing. "Food or fireworks."

Noelle licked her lips. "Good thing you don't have to decide tonight," she said. "Everything you want is right here."

He hummed a response, his smile appearing and disappearing. "Yes," he murmured. "It would seem that way. Too bad I can't really have it all."

She looked up and away, gazing at the sky while her heart beat hummingbird-fast in her chest.

When she dropped Lex off at his car, Noelle didn't want to see him go.

"Thank you for giving me so much of your day," he said. He had his shirt on again, but there was sand in his hair, scattered across his neck and over his arms, a dusting of silver powder on the lean perfection of his body. "I hope we can do it again."

"Maybe," Noelle said, just to be contrary.

She wanted very badly to see him again. But this man, another chance to see him, sounded like a miraculous thing that she should not, could not, have.

"I had a great time," he said. "And I suspect you did too." His smile was pure confidence as he took out his phone. "Let me get your number in case you want a repeat performance."

No. Beautiful days and beautiful men like this never happened to her once, much less twice.

Noelle was about to dismiss Lex and tell him not

to worry about exchanging numbers. But when she opened her mouth to tell him she'd see him around, her number fell out instead. He quickly tapped it into his phone. A few seconds later, her cell vibrated once in her purse. He'd just sent her a text.

"Drive safe," she said. "Don't get too distracted looking up at the sky."

"The one natural beauty to distract me tonight is about to drive away in her little red Honda," he said. "I'm good." Then he lightly touched her arm. "See you soon."

She was both surprised and disappointed when he didn't angle in for a kiss. Instead, he slowly backed away until a foot of space separated them, then two...

"Okay. See you." Noelle waved, feeling awkward, as if they hadn't spent nearly eight perfect hours together.

She got into her car and pulled out her phone to see what Lex said in his text. A fireworks icon. She smiled. When she looked up, his car was still there, waiting with the windows down. He was a sinfully beautiful silhouette in the driver's seat, watching her, not fiddling with a phone like she'd been doing. The lights of his car flashed. "I'm not leaving until you do," he called out.

She put her phone down and started her car. Her phone vibrated again.

You should lock your car door if you're going to sit in a dark parking lot. I'd feel guilty if you got kidnapped.

"I'm going!" she yelled out the window.

His smile flashed at her in approval as she pulled out of the parking lot, making sure to pass within a

few feet of his big, black car. He was almost as bad as
Margot when it came to her safety. The thought passed
through her mind, a fleeting thing, as she drove toward
her house. Despite her innate pessimism, she indulged
in memories of their near-perfect day. His smiles, the
way he looked wading out of the water toward her, the
imagined warmth of his mouth on hers. Noelle fully
expected him to follow her down into her dreams and
stir her mercilessly with desire while she slept.

That night, though, she dreamed about Eric instead
of Lex.

*The wedding was perfect. Sunshine blessed the
very grass under Noelle's feet as she walked across
the gleaming green lawn toward the altar where Eric
waited with the priest, his back to her. She recognized
the long and elegant rod of his back, the way the suit
fit every lean line of him. And she was happy. But part
of her remembered that he'd left her, that he didn't
love her, and screamed for her to stop walking. But
the grass kept moving under her delicate white flats,
the tulle of her dress floated around her and the salty
breeze off the water smelled like paradise. Her dream
self felt content. Noelle recognized that joyful feeling
as something far away from her real self but strong
and undeniable in the heart of the girl who walked in
the dream.*

Turn around. Go back. He doesn't love you. He'll leave!

*But the dream Noelle walked on. Blissful and oblivi-
ous. Only a few feet away from him, she paused to take
in a deep and ecstatic breath, savoring the beauty of
the moment, the sun on her skin, her fiancé being right*

where he promised he'd be. Her chest was full to bursting with contentment.

Then she started forward again, gliding across the grass, the hem of her dress gathered in her hands so she would not fall. As she drew closer, though, she realized that with every step Eric's body became more and more transparent, slowly disappearing before her eyes. She started walking faster. She could see the priest through his body. She reached out to him. Called his name. But he didn't turn around. Her foot touched the grass next to his and she reached out just as he disappeared like he'd never even been there.

Noelle woke up crying.

Chapter 7

Lex felt like the worst kind of bastard.

The wind brushed his face as he drove with all the windows down, the stereo blasting Kid Cudi. The night was too beautiful for what he had done. Noelle. Opening up to him like a flower long hidden in shadow, her reluctant laughter, the way her skin begged him to touch even as her mouth told him not to. Lex wanted to seduce and be seduced by her. He wanted to pull her down into the sand and kiss her under the blast of fireworks until neither of them knew whether the explosions were up in the sky or between them. None of that had anything to do with Margot. Yet it had *everything* to do with her.

When did his desire to shield himself and his parents from the truth of what he'd done turn into the necessity of hurting someone else? Because, make no mistake, someone was going to get hurt. Not just someone. Noelle. Because even though he could lie to himself all night long and say this was just a game they could all laugh about later, the honest part of him saw the wreck that would eventually happen. Noelle would be the one left hurting, and she would never forgive him.

Dammit.

He growled out his frustration. Banged his fist on the steering wheel. The Charger swerved and the car next to him honked sharply. He nearly overcorrected the car into a ditch.

Now he was just being stupid. Lex tapped the phone icon on his steering wheel.

"I'm coming over," he said when Adisa answered.

She paused. "How long?"

He glanced at the car's dashboard clock. "About fifteen, maybe twenty."

"Okay. I'll break out the scotch."

It took him fifteen minutes to make it to his sister's doorstep. He let himself into her house with his key and called out her name as he walked through the darkened living room of her ranch-style Coral Gables house.

"I'm out back!"

Except for the lights in the pool, it was dark in her backyard. But he could clearly see Adisa sitting in one of the chairs near the pool, a yellow robe draped over her already wet bikini. A pair of wineglasses, only one of them empty, sat on the edge of the pool. Lex almost felt guilty.

"Did I interrupt something?" He asked out of politeness's sake, knowing that if he had someone over and his sister called to say she needed him, he would have asked them to leave too.

"Nothing that can't be postponed."

Adisa gave him a glass of his favorite scotch, a true indulgence at more than a thousand dollars a bottle and something she kept on hand because he liked it. He rolled up his pants, sat down and put his feet in the pool. The scotch was smooth going down, a slow and deep warmth worth every single one of its fourteen years.

Adisa already had her own glass. She balanced it on the edge of the pool before slipping off her robe and getting into the water. Her movement provoked ripples in every direction, the lights under the water bright on her white bikini and long legs. She held the glass of scotch above the water as she made her way close to Lex in the shallow end, snagged a passing floaty chair and rested her drink in its cup holder.

"What's got you so glum?" she asked.

He waved his feet back and forth in the water. "I'm not glum, just regretting a few decisions right now."

"You mean that tattoo you got when you were eighteen?" The ice in her glass rattled as she took a sip of the scotch. "I told you that was a crap idea. Only serial killers get dragons tattooed across their entire backs."

He didn't even have a token smile for her at the old joke. The tattoo was something he'd gotten the night before being shipped off to Jamaica. She'd gotten a smaller one in solidarity.

"I messed up," he said.

She rolled her eyes. "What's her name?"

He stopped moving his feet. "What are you talking about? I didn't say anything about a woman."

"Yeah. But you're doing great at work. Mama and Daddy still love you despite everything, and you didn't call me from jail, so it must be a chick. Simple deduction. Tell me I'm wrong."

God... Sometimes he hated that she knew him so well.

"It's not really a…" He stopped the lie before it properly started. "Remember that woman I worked for when I was in Jamaica?"

"As if I could forget. It's not every day my brother gets talked out of becoming a high-class hooker for bored society bitc—"

He cut her off. "She's here in Miami."

Adisa made a point to finish her sentence and then she frowned as she seemed to rewind his statement in her mind. "Is the world that small?"

"Looks like it. She was at Lola's opening the other day." He took another sip of the scotch and told her what happened after he saw Margot at the gallery.

"Is she blackmailing you?" Adisa's look sharpened and, despite her bikini and pretty face, she resembled nothing less than a shark in that moment. "Because if she is, I can take care of that real quick."

Sometimes he worried his sister was more dangerous than she ought to be for a woman raised in silk socks and private schools.

"It's not blackmail. I owe her. You know I do."

"Do you? I think simple logic would've brought you around eventually."

Lex didn't stop the smile that quickly claimed his mouth. Despite everything he'd done, Adisa's faith in him was unshakable. But he wasn't blinded by love like she was. As a kid, he'd been bent on self-destruction. The idea of jail didn't scare him. Threats were like

dares to him. His family's pleas had fallen on deliberately closed ears.

Then Margot happened. The combination of her
ruthless beauty and polished veneer of power had
caught Lex's attention like nothing else. She didn't
threaten him, she didn't beg him. She just told him
how it was. *Promised* him that if he started tricking
out of her club, she would ruin him at school. That was
when he started to listen and they began to be something like friends. Lex owed her a lot.

"Before she came along, it never occurred to me to
just...chill and not be so hell-bent on hurting our parents," he said. "If she hadn't talked to me, I would've
probably done something real dumb like sell Diallo
propriety formulas or something."

"Even back then you weren't that stupid." She
tapped the corner of her glass with a long, purple fin-
gernail. "So, are you going to keep seeing this girl and
pretending you like her?"

"That's just the thing, I do like her."

Adisa gave him a look she must've learned from
their mother. "I hope you know this isn't going to end
well."

"Who you tellin'?" He put his nearly empty glass
on the edge of the pool and leaned back with his palms
flat against the concrete behind him. "Noelle is nothing like Margot thinks she is. I'm not even sure she's
that broken up about the wedding being called off."

"Did she tell you that?"

"No. Just a feeling." He moved his feet in the pool,
enjoying the drag of the water on his ankles. "Even
that day I saw her at the gallery..."

Lex remembered well the heat building in his body,

rising from his thighs, up to his crotch and into his chest. Just at the sight of her. He'd been so lost in his admiration of her body that he was caught off guard when he saw her looking back at him with the same intensity he was sure was in his face. But, in the end, the promise of celibacy he'd made to himself was the reason he hadn't walked across that room and claimed what they both wanted.

He winced as water splashed in his face. Adisa hovered near him, her hand getting ready to splash more water his way.

"Are you going to spontaneously combust over this woman?" she asked with real concern. "I'd prefer you get out of my pool if that's going to happen."

"Don't be nasty," Lex said, getting up to take off his pants and shirt.

He dove into the pool in his underwear, splashing his sister as he went in. Although it was about eighty degrees outside, his sister kept the pool heated. Lex glided under the surface and blew a steady stream of bubbles, swam in front of Adisa, who dipped down to join him, smiling with all her teeth. They circled around each other, holding their breath until Lex felt that panicked feeling of running out of air. But still, he tried to hold out and outlast Adisa. But he couldn't. He burst to the surface with a gasp, spraying water everywhere. His sister shot up a few seconds later, crowing in triumph.

"Good try, big brother!"

He splashed her and swam away. "I almost won this time."

"Keep practicing."

Lex swam the length of the pool to the soundtrack

of Adisa's laughter. Countless laps later, he collapsed on the deck chair and stretched out to stare at the stars. Adisa dropped down next to him, fumbling for her robe and the bottle of scotch.

"It's getting late. I should go."

"You should stay," she said.

Lex turned his head to look at her, starfished on the chair next to his, slowly drinking a fresh glass of scotch and watching him in return. "What am I doing?"

"You didn't come here for advice. You already made up your mind about what to do. I'm not going to waste my breath." Adisa sipped her scotch. "Just be careful, okay?"

"What kind of trouble could I possibly get into? It's not like Margot is the mob or something."

"I can see your trouble coming from a mile away, Alexander. You do too. You're just in denial."

He looked away from her face and its annoying look of *I'm right*. The most sensible thing for him to do was drink more scotch and not think about any of it. So that was what he did.

Chapter 8

"You look like crap."

"Thanks, Margot." Noelle stepped down the last step and into the belly of the yacht and dropped her purse on the low coffee table. Before she left home, she thought she'd looked decent enough in the white minidress and strappy sandals, even if she did have dark circles under her eyes from her sleepless night. Apparently makeup didn't hide as much as she thought.

"If I didn't feel like crap before…" She sat next to her sister and peered over her shoulder through the porthole. Biscayne Bay stretched out, blue and glimmering, beneath the Miami skyline and a jet ski powered past with a steady growl, splashing up water in its wake. The sound of laughter and the clink of glass on glass, a martini shaker at work, loud chatter, came from a room nearby.

Margot dropped a hand on her bare arm. "Are you okay?" Even concerned as Noelle knew she was, her sister sounded cold. But that was simply how she was.

"Yeah," she said with a tired sigh. "I just didn't sleep well last night."

After the dream about Eric, that had been it for her sleep. Instead of staying in bed, she sat on her back porch drinking herbal tea and watching the sun come up. Somehow, with the tea warming her hands, she'd thought about Lex and his offer for her to come over to his place and share a pot of something exotic. It was a euphemism. It had to be. If they'd actually sat in the masculine place where he lived and slept, she wouldn't have been satisfied with just the warm and sweet flavor of the tea in her mouth.

Noelle refocused her attention on Margot just as a look stole across her sister's face, something she was too slow to catch.

"Why didn't you sleep well?" Margot leaned back on the leather bench seat and crossed her legs in the white linen pants, flashing the elegant curves of the matching Louboutin heels. "I thought you had a great date last night."

Noelle had made the mistake of telling Margot about her impromptu date with Lex. Over the phone, her sister had been surprised and then strangely happy for her, saying she was glad for Noelle's new distraction.

"It wasn't really a date," Noelle said. "I told you that on the phone."

Margot shrugged. "A hot guy picks you up at a café and spends the rest of the day with you. I count that as a date."

She narrowed her eyes at her sister. Since when did

Margot approve of any man she ever dated—or even met at a tea shop—without running a thorough background check first? Did Noelle look so desperate she was willing to sacrifice her to some random stranger?

"He could have been a serial killer for all you know," Noelle said. "An arsonist. A meth head."

"You watch too much TV," Margot said. "Just because you live in Miami doesn't mean you'll run into a Dexter at every turn in the road."

"It doesn't mean I *won't*. Isn't Miami the murder capital of the United States?"

"Technically that's Flint, Michigan," Margot murmured with an inward look like she was consulting a mental database. "Or Chicago if you just look at the actual number of murders instead of population percentage."

Noelle didn't ask Margot how she knew that. She took off her shades and anchored them in her hair. The floor shuddered under her feet as the boat pulled away from the dock and deeper into Biscayne Bay.

The yacht party was another one of Margot's ideas, something else to get Noelle out of the house. She hadn't told her sister yet about her dance classes and the people she'd met there, how much better she was feeling about life in general. It would only give her sister another set of people to run security and background checks on. As if anyone who came into Noelle's life was applying for a job and would only pass the test if Margot thought they were worthy.

That was the way of things since their parents died. Noelle hated it. That was the reason she'd had few friends who stayed in her life. Margot investigated them, told Noelle every indecent and awful thing about them until she couldn't look them in the face anymore without seeing their mistakes.

Stella, who was a shoplifter and a girl Noelle had been getting close with in middle school. Allison Mc-Cray and the abusive father she'd shot and blamed on a robbery. Keysha Rodriguez with the lisp and serious cocaine habit. After a while, she'd stopped bringing friends home and then stopped having friends alto-gether. Margot was the one who'd introduced Noelle to Eric. At a party like this one. On a sunny day. It had all seemed perfect, until it wasn't.

Sometimes it was almost a comfort knowing Mar-got had gotten things so wrong.

Other times she just wished Margot would stop med-dling in her life.

"So where is this boat taking us," Noelle asked.

"Somewhere nice." Margot plucked at the hem of Noelle's dress, smiling faintly with her red lips.

Noelle sighed and sank even more deeply into the chair. Her pretense was starting to fall away. Last night's dream had torn her apart while she was living it and now, in the morning, she still felt gutted. The boat ride was a distraction for the moment, but she would have to go home alone at some point to face the pain Eric's memory had stirred up.

She must have been frowning because Margot smoothed her cool fingers across her brow, something she'd done since Noelle was a child. *When you worry, I worry*, Margot always said.

"Is there anything I can get for you?" she asked Noelle now.

"No." She wished there was something to take away the lingering sting of humiliation, the weight of her own weakness and inability to say no when other forces exerted pressure on her life.

Ugh. Enough.

Noelle shook off her unproductive thoughts. "I'm going to get a drink," she said.

"Good." Margot touched her forehead again, a worried look crossing her face before it became blank once more. "There's a bar through there." She pointed toward the short hallway that ended in a room buzzing with conversation.

Noelle didn't feel like dealing with that many people. "Is there one up on deck?"

Her sister hesitated for a moment. "Yes, there is."

"Okay. I'll go up and get some fresh air." She waved toward the hallway where every now and then people toddled by with glasses of liquor in their hands, already on their way to drunk. "This is a little much for me right now." And now she was regretting saying yes to her sister's invitation. She'd wanted company, but not this much of it. "I'll see you later." She left for the stairs.

The dock was about a quarter of a mile away and the boat sailed steadily away from it. Miami's skyline loomed over the water, over Noelle, glittering and decadent. With the sun on her back, Noelle sighed and leaned against the railing, loosening her shoulders once she was no longer belowdecks and subject to her sister's pity.

The party didn't seem like a big one. Maybe twenty to twenty-five people. Despite the beautiful weather, most of the guests were downstairs. But maybe that was where Margot kept the good booze. The boat, probably something that belonged to her sister, wasn't very big compared to the ones she'd seen floating past her during the many years she'd lived in Miami. It was no massive yacht. But it felt like luxury. Leather seats and benches everywhere, a pair of jet skis parked at its rear, gleaming chrome fixtures accenting its modest 120-foot length. *Modest* luxury, Noelle thought with a smile. Only Margot could pull that off and make it seem like nothing.

The bar on deck was relatively quiet. It was manned by one bartender, smiling and shirtless while he flipped a martini shaker in a complicated move that seemed to impress only him. The seven people at the bar barely paid him any attention, only waited patiently for their drinks while chatting among themselves. Three women laughing over their pink-filled martini glasses and already wandering away from the bar, a couple talking intently with their heads bent together and a pair of men leaning against the bar, apparently waiting for their drinks.

Noelle paused with her hand on the sun-warmed metal of the railing. There was something familiar about the man who made up half of the couple. His back was to her, but she knew the way he moved—he lifted his head and laughed, flashed Noelle the strong lines of his jaw, the pink curve of his lips. He leaned even more into the woman who draped her arm around his waist, pressed her cheek against his. They were the same height. Just like Noelle. Apparently, he liked his women tall.

Then the woman looked up, still smiling, and caught Noelle's eye. The woman was beautiful. Smooth skin, her natural hair worn like a crown, flawless makeup. As Noelle stared, curiosity touched the woman's face and then a frown. Noelle's cheeks flamed. Abruptly, she changed course, turning left instead of right to head back belowdecks. Who was the woman with him? How did he know Margot? Was that woman his?

Noelle's hands fumbled on the handle of the nearest door once she made it down the stairs. She pushed her way in, only to stop short at the sight of the couple on the bed, tangled together and half-dressed.

"Sorry!"

She backed out and stumbled into the hallway and to another door. This room was empty. It was small with only a desk and chair, and space enough for a twin bed to unfold from the wall. Noelle sank into the chair and pressed her palms to her hot cheeks and swallowed the lump in her throat. Lex was on the boat. He was on the boat with another woman. Noelle pressed her lips shut. Of course, yesterday had been too good to be true.

It shouldn't matter. She took a breath and then another. It *didn't* matter.

After a few minutes, she felt calm enough to leave the room. She stood up just as the door burst open. She jumped back. A woman came through the door. The same woman who'd been with Lex. She looked relieved to see Noelle.

"Thank God you're in here." The woman drew an exaggerated breath of relief and sat on top of the desk.

"Come sit." The woman gestured toward the empty chair.

Noelle shook her head so hard her hair slapped her cheeks. What the hell was this woman up to? "No, thank you. I don't even know you."

The woman offered her hand. "You may not know

who I am, but I saw you upstairs earlier. You were with Lex last night."

Noelle took a step back. Was this going to be somebody warning her off her man? "Look, I didn't know he already had a girl." That bastard.

"What are you talking about? Don't jump to conclusions. This is not an episode of *Real Housewives* or some other crazy mess." The woman leaned over to pat the chair. "Come have a seat and we can talk like civilized people."

Noelle backed up again, moving steadily toward the door. She made her voice firm. "Again, no thanks."

A knock yanked her gaze to the door. "It's me." Lex's voice came muffled through the door.

Noelle drew in a breath to tell him to go to hell, but the woman jumped up and pulled open the door. She ushered Lex in and squeezed past him. "She's in there," she said to Lex and then left.

Lex completely filled the room with his presence. The faint scent of a citrus cologne or aftershave. The alluring length of his body in boat shoes, blue slacks and a white, linen shirt. His ridiculously gorgeous face. Noelle's heart stuttered stupidly in her chest.

Disgusted with herself, she sidled toward the door, but Lex pressed it shut and turned to her. "Stay."

She opened her mouth again to curse him out but found that her heart was drumming hard in her chest with a sense of betrayal she had no right to feel. "Why?" she snapped the question anyway. "So you can tell me that your girlfriend means nothing to you? I don't want your lies."

Lex's brows knitted in confusion. "I don't have a girlfriend."

The sound of a lock clicking home jerked Noelle's gaze to his face as he moved toward her.

Those words were just what she wanted to hear, never mind that what she saw up on deck was completely contrary to them.

"You look beautiful," Lex said. His whiskey-scented breath brushed Noelle's cheek and she shivered. "I thought about you last night."

If she had any doubts about what he meant, the firm and possessive curve of his hand on her hip dismissed them all. She licked her lips, wanting to be reasonable and sane, but she only whimpered when his hand on her hip guided her back into the wall.

"No," she said, although she wasn't sure what she was saying no to.

"You didn't think about me?" He stepped closer, like he was under a spell and couldn't help himself, his eyes focused only on her.

"I didn't," she lied.

Up until she'd fallen asleep, Lex had been wrapped firmly around her every thought. Wondering why she wanted him so much, wondering if she *could* have him, hoping...

He stopped a few breaths from her. "Kiss me," he said.

"What?"

"Kiss me. I can't—"

His mouth was open when she did kiss him. Warm and wet. She groaned and heard him groan too, a beautiful noise that drew her belly tight and pulled heat into her lap. It was madness. He crowded her against the wall until their hips pressed together. He was already hard. She was already wet. It felt all-too-impossibly perfect.

Once she kissed him, he took control. He slid warm fingers into her hair and around the vulnerable curve of her head, held her at the perfect angle for his kisses, for the wet and firm roll of his tongue as he explored her mouth. She groaned again and pressed into him, her center tingling, wanting to open up and receive every inch of him.

What was wrong with her? She never did things like this.

But this was the fulfilled promise in every look they'd shared the day before. The heat in his gaze, the sizzle of awareness along her skin, the pebbling of her breasts when they begged for his touch, his mouth. Frantic. Sweet. Hard. Noelle gripped his wide shoulders, pulling him close as they kissed, as his hips rolled against hers, as she grew wetter. It was the dizzying and mindless want all the books and movies of her adolescence had promised—this needing someone to touch a part of her, any part of her, until she would do something stupid just to have it. Now she could understand why girls got knocked up in backseats, why Juliet forgave Romeo everything, why Olivia couldn't stay away from Fitz.

Lex gripped her thighs, her hips, and she opened her legs instinctively. He fell between them, knocking her back into the wall. Her skirt rode up and he pressed hard against her, the only barrier between them a few thin layers of cloth.

She rocked her hips, rubbing her aching clit against him through her panties, through his jeans, while their mouths slid together, a wet and urgent sound of connection in the room, and her nipples grew tight and aching against his chest. He fumbled between them, his fingers touching her through the thin cloth of her thong and then slipping between the cloth and her...

"Lex!"

Noelle's hitching moan would've embarrassed her if Lex hadn't made an equally loud noise, his mouth sliding off hers to pant hotly in her throat.

"Is this for me?" He traced the moistness of her desire, a finger circling her clit. "Are you wet like this for me?"

"Yes!" She was shameless in her want, opening her thighs wider for him to stop teasing at the edges of her sex and—

"Oh!"

He firmly stroked her clit and she sobbed out loud. Nails raking his shoulders through his shirt. Legs wrapped around his hips, grinding into the firm pressure of his fingers, the wall knocking with her motions. He was hard against her hand, so hard, so good, and she wanted him inside her, she wanted him now. Lex groaned her name, softly bit the slope of her neck and she felt every press of his teeth in the throbbing between her legs, in the tightening of her nipples.

The door handle rattled. Again and again. The sound wormed into Noelle's consciousness. When she realized what it was, she gasped and flinched back from Lex. Her eyes flew open—when had she closed them?—and she remembered the couple in the other room, the tangle they made on the bed when she'd burst in. And the memory of them dominoed, made her remember the reason she had burst in on them in the first place. She flushed with embarrassment and pushed away from Lex, dropped her feet to the floor. Her legs trembled so much she almost fell, but Lex held her up.

"What…?" His mouth was wet, his lashes low over his dazed eyes. The front of his pants was obscene with the proof of his desire. Noelle took a single step into him and then slid away along the wall, wanting to drop to her knees but also wanting to run away.

"I—I can't…" She shoved her dress down, wiping her mouth with the back of her hand. "*This* is not something I do."

The more she talked, the more Lex's eyes seemed to clear. He cursed and turned away from her, adjusting himself.

"I'm going to—" And she slid back the lock, gasping when she stumbled into a couple pressed together in the hallway, just seconds away from what she and Lex had been doing. With her legs still trembling, she blushed and turned around. She needed a drink. But she found a bathroom first, washed her hands, splashed water on her face. The bar was looking more and more like the place she needed to be.

At the bar on the lower deck, the atmosphere was much more social, distracting her from the still-throbbing heartbeat between her legs. The whole room buzzed with conversation, groups shifting to reconfigure themselves even as she walked in. The bar was busy. The bartender, a woman in a tight corset that spilled her breasts out and up for anyone who cared to look, flirted with everyone she poured a drink for, man or woman, and kept up a constant chatter. The room was loud and lively, the perfect place for her to get lost in.

Margot sat in the middle of the white-leather L-shaped couch, a cocktail in hand while equally gorgeous people formed a circle around her, laughing with her at her dry jokes, adding their own opinions about the things she talked about. Once Noelle walked into the room, she knew Margot saw her. Her sister didn't get up, didn't stop her conversation, but her eyes flickered toward Noelle and then away.

She leaned against the bar and waited for the woman to notice her. "A mimosa, please."

Something stronger would've helped to soothe her nerves, but getting drunk wasn't a situation she ever stepped willingly into. She'd rather burn with the memory of what she and Lex had almost done than lose her cool in front of strangers.

The bartender nodded, tossed her a smile. "Of course, beautiful. Let me just finish up here." She mixed up some fancy concoction that looked too strong for Noelle, collected the resulting twenty-dollar tip with a wide smile and then, while making someone else's drink, moved closer to Noelle. "Your choice of champagne?"

"Whatever you have. I'm not picky."

"Whatever the lady says." She slid the finished drink to another woman, who then leaned over to slide a fifty between her lifted breasts. Moments later, a mimosa landed in front of Noelle.

"Thank you," a deep voice behind her rumbled and then a masculine hand dropped a twenty on the bar.

"Thank you, sir," the bartender said with another flirtatious dip of her eyebrows. "Can I get you anything?"

"Not at all," Lex said. "But thank you for offering."

Noelle was frozen on the spot. She felt Lex's heat behind her, his breath at her ear.

"Why did you leave?" he asked.

Another man squeezed in at the crowded bar, trying

to get access to the sexy bartender, and Noelle grabbed her drink and moved out of his way just as Lex took her arm in a gentle grip and led her away from the bar altogether.

"I don't think you have the right to ask me any questions," she said.

The sound of conversation around them felt oddly like a shield, like everyone around them was so involved in their own business that they didn't have time to pay attention to them. Tired of not having *that* conversation, she allowed him to lead her to a relatively quiet corner of the room. On both sides of the wide room, large windows showed their journey across the water, the sunlight and the passing landscape. At the edge of the long sofa, Lex gestured to a square of space and squeezed himself and Noelle in next to a group of five people in deep conversation about a movie being filmed not far from where they lived in Bal Harbour. Noelle easily tuned them out.

"If I don't have the right to ask you any questions, then will you at least tell me what I did wrong?" His voice dipped low. "You felt so good…"

Noelle ignored the instant surge of lust that bolted between her thighs. "I think you have enough people to talk to, don't you?" It was stupid to feel jealous over a man whose name she hadn't known twenty-four hours before.

"These people?" He looked up, managing to gesture toward them with an eyebrow while his attention was firmly focused on her.

"And the woman you were with."

Now he frowned like she was speaking a foreign language. "You mean Adisa?"

YOUR PARTICIPATION IS REQUESTED!

Dear Reader,

Since you are a lover of our books – we would like to get to know you!

Inside you will find a short Reader's Survey. Sharing your answers with us will help our editorial staff understand who you are and what activities you enjoy.

To thank you for your participation, we would like to send you 2 books and 2 gifts – **ABSOLUTELY FREE!**

Enjoy your gifts with our appreciation,

Pam Powers

**SEE INSIDE
FOR READER'S
SURVEY**

For Your Reading Pleasure...

We'll send you 2 books and 2 gifts
ABSOLUTELY FREE
just for completing our Reader's Survey!

YOUR READER'S SURVEY
"THANK YOU" FREE GIFTS INCLUDE:
▶ **2 FREE books**
▶ **2 lovely surprise gifts**

PLEASE FILL IN THE CIRCLES COMPLETELY TO RESPOND

1) What type of fiction books do you enjoy reading? (Check all that apply)
- ○ Suspense/Thrillers
- ○ Action/Adventure
- ○ Modern-day Romances
- ○ Historical Romance
- ○ Humour
- ○ Paranormal Romance

2) What attracted you most to the last fiction book you purchased on impulse?
- ○ The Title
- ○ The Cover
- ○ The Author
- ○ The Story

3) What is usually the greatest influencer when you <u>plan</u> to buy a book?
- ○ Advertising
- ○ Referral
- ○ Book Review

4) How often do you access the internet?
- ○ Daily
- ○ Weekly
- ○ Monthly
- ○ Rarely or never.

5) How many NEW paperback fiction novels have you purchased in the past 3 months?
- ○ 0 - 2
- ○ 3 - 6
- ○ 7 or more

YES! I have completed the Reader's Survey. Please send me the 2 FREE books and 2 FREE gifts (gifts are worth about $10) for which I qualify. I understand that I am under no obligation to purchase any books, as explained on the back of this card.

168 XDL GJ3D/368 XDL GJ3E

FIRST NAME   LAST NAME

ADDRESS

APT.#   CITY

STATE/PROV.   ZIP/POSTAL CODE

K-216-SUR16

"Is that the woman's name?"

"That's my sister's name."

"Sister?"

"Yes."

She fought another flush of embarrassment. If this woman was really his sister… "Well, it looked to me like she's more than that."

"She's my twin sister if that makes a difference of degrees."

Noelle squirmed under his amused regard. She felt ridiculously exposed, her insecurities on full display for him to see. "It—"

"Oh good, you two got the chance to talk."

The sister in question waded out of the group of people to appear at their side. Noelle clenched her jaw to stop herself from blushing and looking away when Adisa frankly met her gaze. The evidence of the *talk* she and Lex had had still clung, wet and viscous, to her panties.

She was, as Noelle paid proper attention to her, eerily similar to Lex. The same deep-gold skin, curving mouth and regal cheekbones. Even that look of restrained amusement that Noelle had thought was Lex's alone. They were like two gorgeous peas in a pod.

"I see you've got things under control, Alexander. I'll leave you to it." The sister, Adisa, turned to Noelle. "Maybe later on you and I can have that chat." She patted her brother's shoulder and then was gone.

She was apparently a master of dramatic exits.

After several heartbeats, Noelle met Lex's amused gaze.

"So…you were jealous." Lex's mouth twitched.

"No. Of course not." But even to her own ears, she

didn't sound convincing. Noelle rolled her eyes at herself. Even before she kissed Lex, she'd felt drawn to him enough to claim him, despite knowing what was blossoming between them had little chance of becoming anything. She felt like such an idiot.

"There's nothing wrong with being jealous." Lex's mouth twitched again, probably on the verge of full-out laughter at her. "I've felt it a few times myself."

"Not about people you just met, I bet." Noelle tried to relax enough to make fun of herself. It wasn't working yet. She sipped her mimosa.

"Occasionally," Lex said, leaning close until their shoulders overlapped. "I can picture myself getting jealous over you." His skin was sun-warmed, his arms firm through the linen shirt he wore. White looked good on him. The thin shirt was loose over his wide shoulders and subtly sculpted chest. Noelle curled her fingers as the memory surfaced, slick and hot, of what it felt like to touch him. "Like if you left the party with him over there." Lex tilted his head toward a musclebound man, typically Miami-pretty with thick hair and a body poured into tight jeans. A man who was obviously his boyfriend—husband?—leaned close enough for him to kiss.

"I'm not looking for a threesome today," Noelle said, deciding then to go along with the flow of his humor. It was safer than dwelling on what had nearly happened between them a few minutes before.

"Not today then, but how about tomorrow?" Lex teased.

"I can't predict the future."

He nodded thoughtfully. "I'll keep that in mind."

"What…?" She rewound their conversation in her

mind. She'd been kidding! "Why would you—?" She shook her head, smiling. "Never mind." Served her right. She was the one who had started this, after all.

Lex plucked the mimosa out of her hand and tasted it. "Those activities sometimes require a healthy dose of alcohol to get started." He handed back the champagne flute. "You'll need more than that if you hope to change the day's outcome."

"I don't. Thanks very much." She felt herself smiling at his ridiculousness, and that was when he smiled in return, his beautiful mouth spreading wide over square, white teeth that were slightly crooked on the bottom. Foolishly, she'd thought she couldn't find him any more attractive. Noelle cleared her throat.

"So...one of your sisters, huh?"

He laughed at her obvious deflection. "Yes. One of four."

"Are they all as pretty?"

"Of course. According to my parents, the girls are the most beautiful in all of Miami."

"They're probably not wrong."

Lex shrugged, but she wasn't fooled by his nonchalance. He probably thought the same thing. Noelle sighed and chewed the inside of her lip. "I'm glad she's your sister. Obviously, we just met and this thing—" she gestured between them "—may not go anywhere, but if you decide you don't want to see me anymore, or you aren't feeling me at all, just let me know. I like to know where I stand. Okay?"

"Okay." A muscle flexed in his jaw.

She nodded and breathed out, shifted her shoulder where it rested against his. The conversation around them was almost soothing, a background to the low-grade anxiety she'd felt earlier from being among so many people. Now she wanted to rest her head on Lex's shoulder and stay there until the boat ride was over. Maybe try and make up for some of the sleep she lost the night before. That dream...

Noelle twirled the stem of the champagne glass between her fingers and tried to keep her frown at bay.

"Are you feeling okay?" He leaned into her, lightly bumping her shoulder and bringing the crisp scent of his aftershave even closer.

She frowned at the question that seemed to come out of nowhere. "Yes, I'm...I'm good." She passed the warming glass from one hand to the other. "Why? Do I look that bad?"

"You look beautiful." His gaze caressed her body as if her beauty was a given and not the topic up for discussion. "You just look a little haunted."

An interesting choice of words. "It's nothing," she said. "I just didn't sleep very well last night."

"Bad dreams or bad mattress?" He teased. Noelle breathed in at the sight and smell of him so close. His pale brown eyes watched her with concern, a soft tenderness. Her shoulder blade rested on the hard ridge of his chest, a slight overlap of their bodies on the bench, the two of them crowded on both sides by strangers. She felt him breathe, the steady rise and fall of his chest, a tickling exhalation of breath on her cheek.

She was falling in love with him.

A sigh floated past Noelle's lips. She stared into the champagne flute holding the rest of her mimosa. The drink tasted like orange juice with barely a hint of champagne. The only intoxicating thing she'd had all day was Lex's kisses. She drained the glass.

"Bad dreams," she sighed. "I—"

She broke off when a woman suddenly dropped in Lex's lap, flopping her legs on top of Noelle. A white jumpsuit clung to the woman's every curve and her sleek black bob looked fresh from the salon. She smelled like a few too many Bloody Marys, all tomato juice and spice.

"Hey there, handsome!" She draped her arm around Lex's neck and he drew back to look at her face. Or to get out of kissing range.

"I don't think I know you," he said, his face going blank. His version of polite interest, Noelle assumed.

"Not yet." The woman slurred and moved to kiss Lex's cheek. He moved again, graceful and gracious at the same time. "I'm Christine," she said.

"Normally it would be my pleasure, Christine—" Noelle gave him a look "—but I'm a little busy right now. I'm already chatting with a very lovely lady."

Christine looked at Noelle as if she had just noticed her. Noelle wiggled her fingers at the drunk woman.

"Oh my God!" Christine slapped her hand over her mouth, her eyes wide enough to make her eyeballs look in danger of popping out. "I'm *so* sorry."

The people on either side of Noelle and Lex stared at them with amusement. A girl who looked nearly as drunk as Christine, but who had her arms full with her own man, giggled into her martini glass. They didn't even pretend not to be staring.

"I don't blame you for appreciating him, Christine," Noelle said, trying for diplomatic. The woman didn't seem like she meant any harm. "He *is* a cutie."

Christine drew in a drunken breath and leaned toward Noelle, looking excited. "He is! I think he's the cutest straight man in here." Her whisper was loud enough to be heard halfway across the boat.

Noelle played along. "You have excellent taste."

"Okay. I guess I'm going to leave now." Christine's pink-lipsticked mouth drooped. She looked at Lex and then levered herself off his lap and back into a standing position on her high heels. "Have fun!" Then she tottered off to another part of the boat, attracting the stares of almost everyone nearby. "Well…" Noelle raised an eyebrow at Lex, who just shrugged. "Does that kind of thing happen to you often?"

"To my brothers, mostly," he said. She noticed he didn't quite answer the question.

"I don't even know how my sister knows someone like that," she said. Margot was the very opposite of "that drunk girl at the party." And with the history of their parents' relentless partying and Margot's currently uptight…everything, Noelle would think she'd avoid even being in the same room with those kinds of people.

"Your sister?" Lex asked.

"Yeah, Margot. You saw her at the tea shop where you and I met. This is her party. At least I think so. She dragged me here so I wouldn't be sitting in the empty house depressed all day." Noelle clamped her teeth over her lower lip. Why did she just say that?

"Why would you be depressed?" Lex's thigh shifted against her as he turned the full power of his autumn eyes on her. "Because of your bad dream? Or was it something I did last night?" Concern wrinkled his forehead and Noelle gave in to the urge to smooth it away, brushing two fingers over his eyes like Margot often did to her.

His lashes flickered down when she touched him.

"No. Nothing you did," she said. She dropped her hand back to her lap, fondling the stem of the champagne glass. "I..." Was it worth telling him? Noelle licked the corner of her mouth. The dream threaded briefly through her mind, Eric disappearing as she reached out to him, her desperate screams, the feeling that the real Eric had never been in her life at all.

"I got dumped a year ago." She shrugged and tried to make it seem like nothing. "It was hard."

"You still want him back?" Lex's frown returned, along with a hint of concern in his eyes.

"God, no!" But how could she explain the muck of self-doubt that Eric had left behind for her to wallow in? "I thought I was better than the person he left behind." Before Lex could ask her to explain, she continued. "He said some things to me at the end that made me doubt my own strength. I just haven't gotten over it."

"The opinion of a guy dumb enough to leave you at the altar doesn't even rate," Lex said.

Now it was Noelle's turn to frown. She hadn't said anything about Eric being her ex-fiancé. "How did you—"

But Lex tapped a finger on the stem of her empty glass, already standing up. "Do you want another one of these?"

The loss of his warmth against her side distracted Noelle from what she was saying. "Um...actually, I'd like something a little stronger."

A smile darted across Lex's face, something too sharp and fast to be genuine. "Then let's go see if we can satisfy you." He helped her to her feet.

At the bar, she ordered a gin and tonic while Lex got himself a Hennessy on the rocks. The yacht purred steadily beneath them, taking them to some destination Noelle didn't care about.

"Maybe they're giving us a drive-by tour of the island," Lex speculated after Noelle made a throwaway comment about their supposed destination. "Marvel at the awe and mystery that is the Miami land dweller as they guzzle thousands of dollars and roast in the sun." He did a pretty good impression of that guy who hosted *Lifestyles of the Rich and Famous*.

"There you are!"

Noelle turned at the sound of Margot's voice. It took a few moments to see her sister, although once Margot appeared, neatly passing between anyone who dared to block her path, Noelle wondered how she could have missed her. Her white pantsuit, power heels and narrow-eyed beauty were hard to miss or to dismiss.

"That's my sister, Margot," she said, turning to Lex.

He made a noncommittal noise and then touched her back. "That reminds me, I should go find Adisa. I don't want her to feel like I'm neglecting her."

The woman who'd confronted Noelle belowdecks didn't seem at all like she'd want for company in a crowd like this, but Noelle didn't say anything. "Okay. I'll catch you later."

"Yes. Definitely."

By the time Margot appeared at Noelle's side, Lex was gone, his lean figure swallowed up by the shifting crowd.

"Come, Noelle. There's a law professor from UM I'd like you to meet."

"Seriously?" Noelle stared at her sister. "I'm supposed to be having fun and relaxing here, not caving into more pressure from you about law school."

Margot waved a dismissive hand. "Don't be stubborn. He's really funny and has a niece your age already in the program."

Dammit. Noelle sucked down as much of her drink as possible, barely wincing at the bite of the alcohol and hoping she was good and numb by the time she shook hands with the esteemed professor.

"If I become an alcoholic like Ma, I'm blaming you," she muttered.

Margot stopped and turned on her high heels. "Don't say that."

"What? Don't tell you the truth?" She tugged her hand away from Margot. "Come on, let's get this over with since you're determined to do it anyway." It took a few seconds for her sister to start walking with her again, but what Noelle said apparently didn't affect her too much. She introduced her to the professor with her usual smile, her hand a firm grip on Noelle's elbow while everyone else around seemed to actually be having a good time. After the ordeal was over, she thought of calling Lex's cell phone. But she didn't want to seem too desperate. Not to mention her mood had plummeted to the floor. She wasn't fit company for anyone. Despite her threat to Margot, she didn't get another drink, just found one of the rooms belowdecks and locked herself in its quiet, reading a book on her phone until the boat docked and she could escape back to her apartment.

Margot is a trap waiting to spring, she reminded herself from the dark of her bedroom for the millionth time. *Be cautious around her.* But it was a hard lesson for her to remember.

Chapter 9

"That Margot chick seems a little tense." Adisa swung her legs over the side of the yacht as it coasted back into Biscayne Bay. The skirt of her white dress blew up around her thighs.

"Yeah. She's got a lot going on," Lex said, although it seemed most of her tension came from trying to control Noelle's life.

He understood well enough what it was like to be on the receiving end of such persistent and well-meaning attention. It was annoying. And if Margot wasn't careful, she'd push Noelle away for good.

"Her sister seems cool though." Adisa looked over her shoulder at him, warning in her eyes. "She is really into you. Be careful."

"Careful. Yeah. I know." He'd almost messed everything up when he mentioned the fiancé leaving her at the altar. Normally, he wasn't careless enough to let something like that slip, but she had him turned around in the worst way. With one unexpected touch, her fingers scalding a path over his forehead and down his nose to hover just above his lips, he was ready to coax her into his lap and kiss her senseless. And the few minutes they'd spent in that stateroom, the sounds she made, the slick of her against his fingers… Lex shifted in his pants just from the thought of it. With this *favor*, he'd gotten himself into a hell of a mess.

If Margot hadn't been in the equation, he and Noelle probably would have found their way to each other and started something apart from all this chaos. But here he was. Here they were.

"This is pretty messed up, Lex." Adisa turned back to the approaching dock, the breeze from the passage across the water ruffling the baby hair at her temples.

"You're not telling me anything I don't know," he said.

"Then what are you going to do about it?"

He shrugged, although he knew what he *should* do—hell, what he should've done once Margot made him that proposition. Step back. Stay out of this ruthless campaign to steer Noelle's life in a direction of Margot's choosing. Lex stared at the dock until the breeze wrung tears from the corners of his eyes, and he did not look away.

Later that evening, once he was showered and settled on his back porch with a cup of green tea, he called Noelle.

She took a long time to answer, and he was preparing himself to leave a message when her voice clicked onto the line.

"Hello?" She sounded like she had no idea who was calling.

"Noelle, it's me, Lex."

"I know." He heard her sigh through the phone. "What's on your mind?"

The way she spoke was so very different than the joking flirtation they'd indulged in on the boat. It surprised him. Until he remembered how he'd left her. Walking swiftly to the other side of the boat instead of making nice with Margot in front of her. "You," he said. "You're on my mind."

A huff of sound came through the phone. "Am I?" She didn't sound convinced.

Not that Lex could blame her. If it hadn't been for Margot showing up (even though she'd invited him to the yacht party), he would've stayed longer with Noelle, enjoyed whatever pieces of herself she showed him. Maybe get another buzz strong enough to lower his inhibitions and then...

And then what? What else could he do that was worse than nearly having sex with her in an anonymous room protected by the flimsiest of locks? But *damn* he'd been so hard, so desperate for her that he would have begged, had been about to plead on hands and knees, for her to let him finish. Celibacy was harder than it looked on TV.

"Come dancing with me," he said. "You took me to your dance class. Now let me take you to mine."

He could hear her surprise through the phone, another puff of breath, the sound of cloth (sheets?) rustling. "Didn't you say you couldn't dance?"

"I didn't say that I couldn't, only that I don't."

He remembered all too well how free she had been

in the dance studio, moving gracefully to the rhythm of the music, the sweat pouring over her skin and a smile on her face. Even though she didn't say that was why she took the class, Lex could see it was also a chance for her to pay attention to her own body, to use it and stretch it and take her out of her own head. He knew that need.

"So, what do you say? It's no dance studio on the beach, but you can get a good cocktail there. And you don't have to go home at the end of the session unless you want to."

Silence hummed through the phone. When she finally spoke, he wasn't expecting it. "Okay. Why not?" she said.

He felt his smile flash in the dark. Warmed from that glow of gladness he was getting used to feeling just for her.

Instead of getting Lex to pick her up, Noelle wanted to meet him at the club. When she said this, he got all up in his feelings but ultimately understood. They weren't really dating, and there was no point tying the fate of her night to a man who couldn't stay for three minutes and meet her sister. A man who was basically a coward. Lex was trying not to see himself as that, but the evidence wasn't making it easy to stay in denial.

He wanted her. And he wanted to tell her the truth. But, on the phone, he'd sensed a need in her, not for a lover or a man to toy with her feelings but for the release that a sweaty night could bring. And though he wanted her with a kind of teenage desperation, he had a promise of celibacy to keep. That, more than the things he'd said to Margot, made him determined not to touch her. Anymore.

He parked down the street from the club to avoid paying for the unnecessary valet and walked the two blocks to the front door. This was a place Kingsley had recommended, almost too crisp-looking for his taste. But he'd wanted to bring Noelle somewhere nice. The places he liked were a bit grittier. Dirty Miami with reggae music blasting until dawn, a long walk through a dark alley, and maybe fish frying from a cart in the parking lot.

Kingsley's place was fancy. A long line trailed from the club's front door, mostly filled with groups of young and pretty girls, a few couples and men dressed to impress their girl of the night.

Lex stood near the velvet rope and waited for Noelle to get there. A glance at his watch told him he was a little early. The music from inside the club spilled out to the sidewalk, high-energy Top 40 hits with the bass amped up. At the door, the bouncers were tall and muscle-bound, more for keeping an eye on the girls flirting and tipping their cleavage as a passport into the building than for any potential trouble. Even from the outside, the club looked modern and expensive. With the latest sound system and a provocative name in an expensive and well-lit marquee just above the club's entrance.

The name of the club was Pound. Maybe for the pound of flesh you had to give to get in?

He was still pondering the meaning of the sign, half wondering if Noelle was even going to show up, when the low hum of sudden conversation dragged his attention back to his surroundings. At first, he didn't see what the difference was. The line was just as long. The velvet rope didn't open to let anyone new pass. The traffic along the street was steady, an ordinary thing for a Saturday night in Brickell. Then he noticed the bouncers staring down the street and past the line of people waiting at their chance for the golden ticket.

Lex damn near choked on his own breath.

She wore white again. A clingy temptation that began at her collarbones and ended just below her knees. The sleeves of the dress fluttered around her shoulders as she moved. The neckline hung low over her breasts, the loose material draping in a U shape between her breasts and nearly reaching her belly button. Her breasts weren't small. And the material of the dress was low enough that he could safely assume she wasn't wearing a bra. The rest of the dress clung to her, outlining in mouthwatering detail her thick hips and thighs. His mind stuttered at the thought of seeing her from the back.

Wow.

Lex drew in a deep breath and slowly let it out, shoving his hands in the pockets of his jeans to hide the effect just the sight of her had on him. His mind blanked on anything that would prevent him from having her, from inviting her to step out of that dress and into his bed.

"Hey."

That was all he could say. Anything else and he would stutter like a schoolboy talking to his first crush. He curled his fists in his pockets, wishing he'd worn his shirt untucked. A few feet away, the bouncers were blatantly staring at Noelle, barely paying attention to the starved-looking girls in the strips of cloth barely covering their bodies.

"Is this the place?" she asked, gesturing to Pound with a hand holding a tiny purse.

He nodded and cleared his throat. "We can go in whenever you're ready."

"Okay. Let's go." When she turned to head to the end of the line, he pulled her back to him. She smelled like a garden after the rain. "My brother knows the owner," he said. "We don't have to wait."

They made their way past the bouncers and the burgundy velvet rope with no trouble at all. Unless you called every man at the door ogling her body *trouble*. Noelle seemed completely unaware as she walked ahead of Lex and into the club that vibrated with music, a techno version of a song Lex had heard once or twice on the radio. He deliberately kept his gaze above her waist while they walked. He didn't want to trip and fall. At nearly midnight, the club was far from full, definitely not the hot commodity the long line outside made it seem. Strobe lights flashed. The music pounded into his chest and his gut, a heavy pulse. But he didn't know if it was the music or the want for Noelle that made him throb.

He leaned close to her ear, trying to be heard above the sound of the music. "You want a drink?"

She shrugged and stepped equally close to him to reply. "Sure. Just a club soda, though, since I'm driving."

Although Kingsley had a VIP section reserved for them, Lex grabbed their drinks from the bar before guiding her to the glassed-off leather chairs. At the VIP section high above the dance floor and with a view of most of the club, he gestured for her to sit in the curved, red leather bench. But she shook her head, took her club soda and stood by the railing instead.

Her back was to him. And the heavy, heart-shaped curve of her ass in the dress made him adjust himself in his jeans. Her hair, piled on top of her head in a lush cloud and sparkling with some sort of glitter, made her look even more like a goddess among women. Lex sipped his drink, a Hennessey on the rocks, and took a moment to control his breathing before joining her at the railing. He kept at least two inches between them. He didn't know what he would do if they touched.

"This is an interesting place," she said.

Noelle braced her arms on the railing as she looked down into the club. The dance floor was practically empty except for a group of sorority girls, early drunks, dancing up on each other and taking selfies. Their laughter rang out above the music.

"Yeah." *Interesting* was one word for it. His brother was a man who ran in a few different circles. He would be as comfortable here as at the old-school Jamaican bar where their parents spent the occasional Saturday night. The crowd was young and hot, the music nothing special. But the club itself was modern and hard, chrome and steel everywhere, mirrored surfaces reflecting smiles and gyrating bodies. In another mood, Lex could've had fun there.

Next to him, Noelle nodded her head along to the music and sipped her club soda.

"Do you want to dance?" This wasn't the type of music he liked, but he was flexible. Tonight wasn't just about him, after all.

"Not yet. This music isn't really moving me. But I'm

enjoying watching the people." Her eyes dipped over him before going back to the dance floor.

She watched the dancers for a while longer, long enough for two more songs to come and go, long enough to finish her club soda, and then she turned to face him.

"So this is your spot?"

Lex yanked his gaze up from her cleavage, but the look in her eyes made him know she definitely saw him looking. "Never been here before. My brother says women love this place. I think it's the mirrors." He sipped his drink to hide his smile.

Noelle wasn't amused. "You say you like dancing. This place isn't for that. Where do you like to go?"

He hesitated. "It's nowhere like this."

"But they have music we can dance to, right?"

Lex thought about the constant pounding bass, the DJ who hardly ever played a bad song, the inexpensive Jamaican beer and everything else about the club that had kept him there until sunrise more than a few times. "Absolutely," he said.

"We should go there."

He looked around Kingsley's fancy club, impressed with it for what it was, a showplace. Someplace to see and be seen, to listen to music and people watch. Yeah, it wasn't the type of place for him, but it was nice to see it wasn't the type of place for Noelle either.

"All right. Let's go. Get in the car with me or follow."

She bent to put her empty glass on the table, the front of her dress gaping to show the full rise of her breasts. "I'll follow. That seems easiest. Just go slow and don't lose me at the lights."

Lex drained his own drink and slid the empty glass next to hers. "It's not too far."

The club was barely fifteen minutes away, a winding ride through two Miami neighborhoods that brought them into a place that straddled the rich and middle class, the club a leftover from pre-gentrification days that managed to stay in business despite the rising taxes. It also helped that the guy owned the building. No landlord to kick him out in favor of charging hipsters three times the rent.

The place, whose name no one remembered, was the same as always. The parking lot overflowed at one in the morning. Someone pulled out just as he pulled in, but he left the spot for Noelle and exited to circle the surrounding residential neighborhood for a place where he wouldn't get towed.

The night was warm and dark, street lamps lighting the path winding past houses too rich for his blood. Lex strolled through the silenced neighborhood, hands in his pockets while the palm trees rustled from the wind's passing.

This time, Noelle was the one waiting for him at the entrance to the club. At the wide archway that led into the building, she stood in her seductive white, one hip hitched as she took in her surroundings. The low, one-story building. Potholed parking lot. The man in an apron selling fried catfish and fries on the other side of the club entrance. Very different from the scene at Pound.

Lex walked past girls in tight and bright dresses, as well as sky-high heels, who shakily navigated their way through the parking lot and toward the door of the club that had no lines, no waiting, just a pair of security guards, one wanding down each person who wanted to get in, while the other checked IDs.

The hard, driving rhythm of reggae music poured out of the club and put a bounce in nearly everyone's step. Being there was easy and reminded Lex of some college days in Jamaica, nights when he'd escape from the confines of his school and the watchful eyes of his family to find a kind of freedom in a dance hall, an anonymity he could get no place else. Not even in Margot's club.

"This looks more like it." Noelle threw a smile at him over her shoulder as she pulled her ID from her cleavage and turned it over to the security guard. She'd purposely left her purse in the car. The guard gave her license a brief look but damn near memorized everything about her body and face.

Lex watched him with annoyance but kept any sign of it from his face. The opening beats of a classic Sly and Robbie song pulled them into the heart of the club and Noelle walked in ahead of him, snapping her fingers and twitching her hips to the rhythm. Although he knew what to expect, Lex gave the place a quick glance, trying to imagine it through her unfamiliar eyes.

The low ceiling was either intimate or stifling, depending on how you looked at it. The multicolored string lights hanging from the ceiling and around doorways, even the bathrooms', looked like the sad remains of Christmas that the last family on the block never took down. Darkness hid most sins of the place—its chipped bar, painted concrete floor, the DJ who looked old enough to have grandkids but still knew what it took to get people onto the floor.

But Noelle didn't seem to mind or see any of that. Just walking in, she seemed to loosen up, the tense height of her shoulders relaxing, her body becoming more fluid. Sexier. And if he hadn't noticed the slow unwinding of her tension, Lex wouldn't have realized she'd been carrying around a weight on her shoulders.

Under the guise of offering to buy her a drink at the relatively quiet bar, Lex wanted to ask what was wrong. But before he could lean in to suggest the bar, she pulled him toward the crowded dance floor. "Come dance with me."

He went. A flicker of surprise crossed her face as he followed her without protest.

"You're actually going to dance with me?"

"Yeah. Were you just asking to be polite?"

"No, no." But the look on her face said otherwise. Then she rolled her eyes. "None of that matters. I haven't heard this song outside my house in a long time. Come."

Once they were on the packed dance floor, making room for themselves among the sensually moving bodies that smelled of sweat and hair lotions and every kind of cologne and perfume, Noelle slipped into the rhythm of the song like she didn't care whether or not Lex joined her. She slowly rocked her body to the beat, her arms rising in the air, eyes falling shut.

The DJ slipped into "Heads High" from Mr. Vegas and Noelle smiled like she'd heard the voice of an old friend.

Lex was hard from the first bass beat. The sinuous movement of her body was hypnotic. Sexual. And he had to stop watching her, had to start moving too, otherwise he would embarrass himself all over the front of his jeans. The bass settled in his chest, in his hips, moving him to the thudding rhythm of the song.

Although it had been weeks since he'd made time to go dancing, he fell into it as naturally as he breathed. Before he started working for Margot, Lex had already loved to dance. Merengue, bachata, dancehall, even a little modern dance. But it was only once he started taking his clothes off for money that he actually fell in love with the sheer physicality of movement. With the way his body could seduce without him touching someone else.

And although it was the worst idea he'd ever had, he wanted to seduce Noelle.

She was off-limits. He wasn't having sex right now. Margot would kill him.

But none of that mattered. He fell into the beat of the music and it caught him, snaked through his body, rocked his hips with unsubtle intention. He danced close to Noelle but did not touch her. He felt eyes on him, roaming his body as sweat poured down his face and stuck his already thin T-shirt to his back and chest. He felt hot enough to burn down the entire club.

One dance later, maybe two, Noelle opened her eyes, licked them up and down his body, a smile curving her wet, red lips. Sweat glowed against her face and throat under the multicolored lights.

"Where'd you learn to dance like this?" she asked, breathless and sinuous against him.

Lex knew he answered with words but didn't listen to himself speak, only groaned into the trail of heat her eyes left over him. Her nipples were hard points against the front of her dress and he licked his lips, imagining them tight and straining under his tongue.

The music sped up, segueing into Rupee's "Tempted to Touch."

"Come here," she said with a sly smile and the curl of one finger.

Noelle became a different person when the music moved through her. It wasn't the athleticism or showmanship of the dance studio, but her whole body moved in a way that made his mouth dry. He was still hard, but he ignored it just like he ignored the sweat dripping down his body. Lex licked his lips and moved closer to her. Dancing. Determined not to just push his hips into hers and grind on her like most of the men in the club were doing with their dance partners. He wound his back, his hips, easily recalling the moves that had women throwing bills all over his nearly naked body on the stage in Jamaica.

"You're good at this." Noelle smiled and tossed her head back. Her hairline was damp and above her mouth. Lex wanted to lick her dry and then wet again.

The music grew even faster, reggaeton and then soca and they were dancing together, hips bucking and winding, backs moving lower, chests moving teasingly close then backing up. Noelle licked her lips, dragged her palms down her sweat-slick neck and into the bare valley between her breasts.

Other men watched her. Inched closer to the mesmerizing motion of her bottom. Lex gave a skinny brother who wandered too close a warning glance. Noelle didn't dance pretty or cute. She threw her entire body into the dance when it got good to her, her chest heaving and sweat coating her face, her throat. The music bucked her exquisite body all over the dance floor.

Kat DeLuna's voice panted over the frantic bounce of the music.

Lex was so ready for Noelle he could burst. She slid up to him, jerking her hips, and he snagged her even closer, moving with her, keeping rhythm with her, meeting the challenge of those uptilted eyes, her dark red mouth.

Someone moved suddenly behind Noelle, a woman who was dancing with the skinny guy, and pushed Noelle into Lex. He hissed as the cradle of her hips pushed into his erection.

Noelle's eyes abruptly met his. But she didn't move away even when the woman behind her gave back the space on the dance floor. Instead, she hooked her arms around the back of his neck and his entire body groaned with relief when she stayed exactly where she was, her hips, guided by the music, making tight circles against him. She was hot through their layers of clothes. His jeans, her dress. Their underwear. Arousal spiked through him. If she moved away from him now, he would die. He would honestly explode right then and there. He drew the breath into his mouth with a hiss. She had to know what she was doing to him. Grinding on his hardness. Pressing the heat of her lush body against him.

Lex tried to ground himself with a steadying hand on the small of her back. But he only felt the movement of her waist, the muscles making her move so sinfully well against him. He had to stop this, he had to—

Her hand under his shirt halted every single rational thought. He still danced, but all of him waited for what she would do next. Everything in him hinged on the press of her palm against his stomach. But she didn't stop. With her eyes locked on his, Noelle shoved up his shirt and slid her hand in the sweat over his abs to his pecs. Her nail pressed into his nipple and he felt the thick muscle of his pecs jump under her palm. He bucked against her, growling low in his throat. He leaned his mouth close to her ear.

"You have to stop."

She pinched his nipple.

Lex grabbed her hips. Pulled her into him and across the dance floor. Through the crowd of dancers who gave him knowing looks. But he didn't pay them any mind. His body was making all the decisions for him, guiding her toward the place in the club where more than a few couples often ended up. It was a hidden corner under the speakers, dark and intimate with the throb of the music pounding even harder, the bass shuddering over his skin. Lex pushed her back into the wall and she moved willingly with him, hands around his neck, meeting his mouth in a hot kiss even before her back properly settled into the wall.

Theirs was no tentative press of lips, no hesitant kiss but the instant and devouring opening of mouths. A tongue-sucking, back-gripping, deep-groaning call to mate that shook Lex's thighs, hardened him even more in his jeans. Noelle tasted so damn good. Fresh toothpaste. The faintly waxy texture of her lipstick. She moved with him, grabbing his back as he grasped her hips. They pushed together, groaned as one when she opened her legs and he felt the hot clasp of her thighs, imagined the even hotter grip of her cleft around him. Noelle rubbed her chest against his, her nipples pressing into him through his thin shirt and her thinner dress.

And still they kissed, open-mouthed and wet, only pulling back to gasp for air. All the while, their bodies moved steadily together, hips circling and firm, Noelle's hand under Lex's shirt pinching and twisting his nipple.

Come home with me. The words were right there, ready for him to say.

"Do you want to come to my place?" She met his eyes fearlessly, her mouth lipstick-smeared and wet. Everything in him shouted *YES*.

But Margot. His celibacy. The truth Noelle needed to know before anything else happened between them.

Lex spat a silent curse. "We should take it slow." He cursed himself out with every stupid word he said, knowing he was putting out mixed signals, telling her no when his body was obviously ready for her. "This feels good right now, but I don't think we'll be okay with it in the morning."

The spasm of rejection on her face made him instantly reach out to her. But Noelle stepped back from him and took a deep breath. "You may be right." She rolled her shoulders and straightened the front of her dress. "I think it's time for me to go home. It's getting late."

Lex mentally howled the scream of the damned but eventually jerked his head in a nod. He desperately wanted a drink, and by *drink* he meant the liquor between her thighs. When she turned away to push through the dance floor and head toward the door, he took a moment to press down on the hardness in his jeans. Frustrated pleasure shuddered through him, the rough stimulation only adding to the ache of wanting her. He followed her.

In the parking lot, Noelle pulled the single key from where she'd stored it in her cleavage. Lex eyed the swell of breasts. Where did she have room for that *and* her ID? But she was already opening her car door.

"Thanks for inviting me out tonight," she said.

It was impossible not to notice she'd said nothing about having a good time. *Both of you could have had an even better time*, a voice whispered in Lex's head.

"Thank you for coming with me."

Then an awkward silence settled between them.

"Well, I'll—"

"It's—"

They both started talking at the same time and then stopped at the same time. It was painful.

"Drive safely," he said after it looked like she wasn't going to say anything else.

"Yeah, you too."

Her leg disappeared into the car and the door slammed shut. She wasted no time in starting the car and pulling out of the parking space, forcing Lex to step out of the way or risk getting run over.

That was stupid. He was stupid.

Lex lingered in the parking lot, the music from inside the club thudding its insistent beat, although it wasn't as loud from outside. He thought about going back inside but then dismissed the idea nearly as soon as it came. The music was good, as always, but, even this far away from the big homemade speakers, the sound of the heavy bass only made him think of Noelle and the feel of her pressed against him, thick-thighed and wet-mouthed, her nipples swollen with want, begging him to touch them.

Come to my place. Her words echoed inside his head.

The ring of them followed him all the way to his car, during the drive home and through the front door of his house. When he lay on the bed, naked and damp from his shower, her invitation echoed still.

Do you want to come to my place?

How he wanted to say yes. Could easily imagine giving her the answer they both wanted and allowing the night to run its natural course. He licked his lips and imagined it all in hip-jerking detail.

But, no, that couldn't happen.

This has to end, he thought. He couldn't do this to himself or to Noelle another night. He had to tell her the truth.

Chapter 10

Lex wanted to look Margot in the face when he told her that Noelle was suffering more with her meddling than without. He called her to meet up after work at the same place as last time. He got there first, settling into the booth by the window that had a small postcard propped up in the middle of the table advertising the day's specials. Oxtail and stew peas.

He was worn out from his work day, mentally exhausted and impatient with the code that didn't want to act right. He'd manipulated every variable, came at it from just about every angle, but it still didn't do what it was supposed to. Maybe he just needed to step away from it, come back with a fresh perspective. His forced manipulation wasn't working. Maybe he needed to just chill and let it tell him what it needed. The irony of his sudden decision wasn't lost on him.

Margot needed to leave Noelle alone, let her have her life in peace.

But what did that mean for any relationship he hoped to have with Noelle?

He clenched his jaw, arms stretching out on either side of him on the back of the booth.

The restaurant was more than half full with the after-work crowd, some settling in to avoid traffic with a beer and a full meal while others ate patties out of the white bags and watched the pedestrians pass by.

Lex was watching slow-moving vehicles and thinking about Noelle when he saw Margot walking toward the restaurant. She was immaculate in a white pantsuit. A tall woman with a confident stride, too skinny and with enough attitude to put off any man who even thought of talking to her. She saw him through the window and dipped her head in acknowledgment before making her careful way over the threshold and into the restaurant. People turned to stare, but she didn't seem to notice.

"Alexander." She looked tense as she sat down, the corners of her mouth pinched tight.

"You look a little pent-up," he said. "You want a drink?"

She flashed him a look that said she was far from amused by him. "No, nothing alcoholic, but I could use a ginger beer." She looked around for the waitress and waved her over when she caught her eye. "I'm not hungry, but I could use something to tide me over until my dinner meeting tonight."

"That's a late meeting. Hopefully it's not all business."

She ignored his less-than-subtle inquiry into the

state of her love life and ordered a ginger beer from the waitress once she came over, pretty in her jeans, Red Stripe–beer tank top that bared her belly and a tattoo of a naked woman rising up her hip. She gave Lex an appreciative once-over but otherwise kept it professional.

"A ginger beer for me too, please," Lex ordered when it was his turn.

The young girl, who looked like she was still in college, swished away to put in their orders.

"I see hanging out with Noelle hasn't dimmed your appreciation for other women."

Was she irritated on Noelle's behalf? "I'm not blind," he said. "But I'm also not seeing anyone else right now. Noelle is it." He braced his forearms against the edge of the table. "Since you brought it up, I don't think your sister needs your help."

"You said that before and I still disagree," Margot said.

"Your disagreement doesn't make it any less true. That guy may have screwed her over, but he didn't destroy her. You were wrong about what she needs, and what she wants." *Like when you said she doesn't have a sex drive.*

Lex shifted in the booth as he thought exactly about where that sex drive of hers had almost brought them.

The waitress came back with their order and Lex immediately took a long pull from his ginger beer, the fizz and bite of the soda on his tongue a welcome distraction from the memory of the club.

"Why are you saying any of this?" Margot poured her ginger beer into a glass and daintily sipped from it with a straw. "She seemed happily distracted on the boat."

"I've talked to her for more than a few minutes at a time and actually listened to what she's saying." He gave her a meaningful look and felt a momentary sense of triumph when she squirmed. Lex sighed. He took another drink before he said anything else.

"Noelle is a grown woman," he said. "She's not some rare flower ready to get blown away by the slightest breeze. Obviously she's dealing with issues from that man who didn't have the good sense to hold on to a good thing when he had it, but who wouldn't?"

Now it was Margot's turn to give him a look. Suspicion flared in her dark eyes. "A good thing?"

"Your sister is a good woman—" *A fine-ass woman*, Lex thought, but he tactfully left that part out. "Any man with eyes and a brain knows she's got a lot going for her. I'm not saying anything you don't know."

Margot crossed her arms on the table. She looked as implacable as always, ready to double down on an opinion she absolutely believed in. "The whole point of having you *escort* her around town—" Lex winced at the word "—is to make her feel good about herself and forget about that damn man who broke her heart."

"That's just it—her heart may have been broken, but she isn't. You don't need me to spy on her and give her something she doesn't need. She's fine."

"You don't know her as well as you think you do."

"You don't know her as well you should."

Her glass of ginger beer settled on the table with a thump. "That's not very nice."

"You don't care about *nice*. You care about truth, and that's what I'm giving you. Noelle is fine. I don't need to show her a good time or any foolishness like that." He paused, remembering their night at the club. "She has no trouble finding men to date or whatever."

Margot's head tilted as suspicion narrowed her eyes. "Did you sleep with her?"

Lex was surprised she had just now gotten around to asking him that question. "No. I didn't." He left it at that.

She blew in a sigh, carefully watching him. "Obviously you don't have to continue with this if you don't want to, but I think she still needs that…buttress to her self-esteem."

"She doesn't. The last thing she needs is fake support. Actually…" He paused when his phone vibrated in the breast pocket of his blazer. Frowning, he pulled it out to glance at the incoming call but didn't answer. "I want to tell her the truth."

"What truth?" Margot asked. Her upraised eyebrow chided him for looking at his phone during their conversation, but Lex ignored her. He wasn't a naive kid anymore, nervous about pissing her off with his less-than-polite manners.

"Don't play dumb," he said. "It doesn't suit you." He put his phone facedown next to his plate. It vibrated once, a notification that he had a new voice mail.

"Well, suddenly turning up the noble gentleman doesn't suit you either."

Lex turned from the phone to give her his full attention. "Really? What are you saying exactly?"

She shook her head, pinched the bridge of her nose. "I don't know what I'm saying. Alexander, she's my little sister. I'm worried for her. I want to give her the best of everything, the best opportunity, the best love."

"Some things she has to find for herself. You can't smother her with love and expect her to embrace it like it's not squeezing the life out of her."

"You've become quite the uh…Dr. Phil since Jamaica."

Margot's comment didn't even deserve a reply. In response to his silence, she also fell quiet, thoughtfully sipping from the glass of ginger beer, her lips closed tight around the straw. Finally, she seemed to make up her mind about whatever was tossing around in that brain of hers.

"Go ahead and pull back from seeing her. Let me just talk to her and see how she's doing. Give me a little while to check in on her before you tell her anything." Then she frowned again, her red lips drawing into a thin line. "Where is all this coming from anyway?"

"I told you, she's an incredible woman. She deserves more than to be manipulated like this." He considered telling Margot that he was genuinely interested in Noelle and he wanted to take her out on dates that weren't interrupted by the phantom of her overbearing sister. But he kept his mouth shut. "Okay. I won't say anything to her. Not right now, but you need to think about how to resolve this whole situation. I thought doing this favor would make me feel better, but instead I feel like a total shit. This almost feels like something that the old me would do."

And as he said it, Lex realized it was the truth. As an idiot boy in Jamaica, he used his body and his charm to get what he wanted and didn't care about the collateral damage. Maybe the only difference was that he often found women to play with who were like him and didn't look beyond the evening or the afternoon. The pleasure was shared and then it was a memory, leaving nothing worth holding on to. A feeling of sickness roiled in Lex's stomach.

Lex blindly reached for the bottle of ginger beer and drank the rest of it in long, necessary gulps.

"Are you okay?"

"Not really."

Lex signaled the waitress for the check and then, once it came, quickly paid it.

"I wish I could say it was good to see you again, Margot." He walked her to the door and out to her car.

"It's a good thing this isn't the first time I've heard that," Margot said, "or I'd take offense."

"I'm probably the least offensive guy you know," he said and closed the door of her black Benz. "These days, anyway."

Margot smiled faintly at him, though her eyes remained cool. "I'll see you again soon."

She started her car and put it in gear. Lex turned to head to his own car and did not watch her drive away. Instead, he pulled out his phone and redialed his last incoming call.

"Hey," Noelle's voice came warmly through the phone. "I hope I didn't interrupt something."

"Nothing important." He started walking toward his car. "What's up?"

"Come to dinner with me this weekend," she said.

As she talked, his footsteps slowed and then stopped. He stood in the parking lot with the phone held loosely to his ear. "After what happened the other night, I didn't think..." He didn't know what else to say about that night of regrets. "Never mind. Sure, dinner sounds great. Any place in mind?"

"Yes."

She gave him the name of a restaurant his sister Alice was always raving about and he said he'd meet her there at seven o'clock on Friday evening.

"No," she said. "Come pick me up."

Lex was so surprised he almost missed the address she rattled off. "Oh, sorry. Tell me your address again."

She repeated the address, laughter threading through her voice. "I'll see you then. Okay?"

What else could he say? "Okay."

Lex showed up too early for their dinner date.

He sat in Noelle's driveway with fifteen minutes to burn, his car off, the phone sitting dark in its cradle, watching the lights in the window of her front room. Tonight, he would tell her the truth. No matter the distraction, no matter what he stood to lose in the process.

The car's dark leather hugged his back and thighs, a comfort while he quaked inside with mild terror. Her front door was barely fifteen feet away. All he had to do was get out, walk those few feet, tell her what he needed to and then let her decide whether or not she wanted to eat with him. His hand reached for the door handle.

He jerked it back when his phone rang, a jarring and loud sound from the car's speaker. Noelle's number and face glowed from the cell phone.

"Is that you sitting in my driveway?" she asked when he answered.

Shit.

In the front room, a pair of slats in the blinds gapped like someone's fingers were holding them apart. Watching him. The car's clock showed he'd been sitting in the silent car for at least ten minutes. He adjusted the air at the back of his throat, fighting his embarrassment.

"I am. Are you ready?"

Her silence was as loud as any laughter. "Sure. Let me grab my purse and lock up."

She stepped out of the house three minutes later at seven on the dot. Although nothing she wore could disguise her body's sensual curves and mouthwatering thickness, tonight's outfit was not as provocative as the one from the last time. This dress, electric blue and sleeveless, sat high over her breasts, revealing not even a hint of cleavage. The skirt was wide and loose and touched just below her knees, fluttering with every step.

Lex got out of the car and opened the passenger side door for her, stepping back to let her pass him. The back view of the dress was not as modest as the front, the cloth allowing for the looser movement of her gorgeous ass, showing the subtle movement of its mouthwatering dip and sway.

"You look good," he said.

She sank into the leather seat and demurely tucked herself into the car, her purse on her lap. "Thank you."

He put Fela Kuti on the stereo, put the car in gear and reversed slowly out of her driveway. Beside him, she was silent and still, her legs crossed and her purse clasped loosely in her hands. Her perfume was subtle, a fruity cloud that made him think of mangoes and bare bodies ripening in the sun.

"It was a pleasant surprise to get your invitation," he said. Although it hadn't really been an invitation as much as it had been an order. One he'd gladly followed.

The faint twitch of her mouth pretty much confirmed that. "Thanks for accepting. I wasn't sure if you were doing anything, had another date or something else going on."

"I would have canceled if I had," he said, realizing it was true.

He felt her eyes on him, weighing and evaluating. "You have really good game," she said.

"I don't want to be a player anymore," he said. The atmosphere was too heavy. Even if he was the one who'd caused it. But Noelle didn't react. Lex sighed. "I wanted to see you. If you hadn't called, I would have."

Noelle nodded. Her red lips pursed and she looked briefly at him, seeming surprised to catch him watching her, before she turned her attention back to the passing scenery. "I'm glad we're on the same page."

Lex swallowed and then slowly breathed out, the guilt working the muscle in his jaw. They weren't even in the same damn book.

At the restaurant, they were a little early for their 7:30 p.m. reservation but still got immediately seated, tucked away in a romantic alcove overlooking a back garden blooming with lavender, sage and rosemary. The lights were suitably dim, provided by a baroque lamp shade made of elegant swirls of copper hanging low overhead. A small vase of yellow daisies sat precisely in the middle of the small wooden table.

Lex raised his eyebrow as he looked around the space. "Your idea?"

"Well, this is a French restaurant. Maybe the romance comes with the price of admission." Noelle settled into the chair opposite him with a graceful shrug.

Seeming completely relaxed, Noelle settled her small purse on a corner of the table and spread the napkin from her place setting across her lap. The soft-ened light settled over her features, the wings of her eyelashes and her shoulders moving elegantly under the straps of her dress. And Lex watched her, looking for traces of the sadness Margot insisted were there. Sure, Noelle seemed thoughtful, and there were times that a hint of melancholy turned down her mouth and made her eyes glisten like diamonds. But nothing she said or did made him think she was ready to chuck it all because of some idiot who had been too afraid of happiness to grab and hold on to it with both hands.

A waitress came, quiet and polite, into their alcove, bringing water and the bottle of red Bordeaux he'd or-dered. She smiled at them both, kind and faintly envi-ous, before leaving with their orders.

Lex waited until the waitress left before he braced his arms on the table and gave her his absolute atten-tion.

"This is a nice place," he said.

"Isn't it? Ruby—remember her from dance class?" When he nodded, she continued. "She told me about it. They have an incredible strawberry-and-Nutella crepe."

"For dinner?"

"Any meal you want."

With a bright smile, quick and completely unex-pected, she reminded him of his youngest sister, Elia, who loved having breakfast any time of the day or night. She could even be a little obsessed with pan-cakes.

"My sister loves pancakes too. She can have them for any meal."

Noelle wrinkled her nose. "Blasphemer. I'm not sure what bad name to call you right now," she said.

"What?"

"I didn't say anything about pancakes. I said *crepes*."

"I heard you the first time. Crepes are just glorified pancakes."

After a moment, she shrugged, the corners of her mouth soft with an almost smile. "I'll have to consider that point."

When the waitress came back with water and warm bread for them to share, they put the crepe argument aside.

"You have a lot of brothers," she said, taking an appreciative sip of her wine. "I can't imagine growing up with that much testosterone in one house."

"It was all right with me, obviously." He shrugged. "I can't speak for my mother and sisters."

He chewed on a piece of buttered bread and watched her with a smile. She was damn beautiful. He would miss this when she was gone from his life.

"Not that I'm not enjoying this very light tiptoeing," he said once he finished chewing, "But you said you wanted to talk to me."

"That's not what I said, but apparently *you* want to talk to *me*."

"I do, but my conversation isn't very urgent." He watched her put another piece of bread in her mouth, the butter melting and leaving a glistening trace on her lips that he immediately wanted to lick off. *Focus.* "After the…uh, unfortunate way our last outing ended, I thought the last thing you'd want to see was my face."

Noelle slid her knife into the butter again but didn't touch the piece of bread already on her plate. Under the dim light, it was hard to tell, but it felt like heat radiated from her, a blush. "I was a little forward the other night at the club, and when I didn't get what I wanted, which was you in my bed, I acted like a brat. I want to apologize. I'm not usually like that."

Lex denied her apology with a quick shake of his head. "No, you have absolutely nothing to apologize for. I was the one who started things up. I...just wasn't ready to follow through."

"I've been around long enough to know that rejecting sex is not the same thing as rejecting the person." Noelle rested her elbows on the table and linked her fingers under her chin. "And I should have been more gracious when you told me no."

This was the most backward conversation Lex had ever had. True, turning down sex wasn't something he did on a regular basis, if ever. If it hadn't been for Margot and the promise he made to her, they would've done a lot more than kiss that night. Speaking of Margot...

Lex thought about what he should say and how to say it. "I really, really wanted to..." He broke off. "I've thought about making love to you since the moment I saw you at the gallery. If you'd wanted to have sex the afternoon we talked at the tea shop, I would've totally been down—" her frown stopped him "—not that that's what you wanted."

A smile lurked at the corner of her eyes. "No, no," she said. "I understand what you're trying to say."

"I promised myself I'd be celibate," he said quickly. *Did I really just...?*

"What?"

Now she was going to make him repeat himself. It sounded so stupid when he said it out loud. "I gave up sex."

Her eyes were wide with a kind of horror. "For how long?"

He shrugged. "I'm not sure."

Noelle stared at him over the rim of her wineglass like he was some sort of museum oddity. "Celibacy." She tasted the word like it was a completely foreign dish, one she had to roll over her tongue several times to make any sense of. "Why? I mean, I'm not questioning your choice, but you seem like a very sexual person. Why are you cutting yourself off if that's not in your nature?"

His tongue hovered between the truth and deflection before he finally chose the truth. "I'm a bit of a ho."

She choked on her wine and laughter spilled past her fingers. "Excuse me?"

The waitress chose that moment to come up to the table. To be fair, she had their food and was just doing her job, but Lex felt a spasm of annoyance that she was interrupting his already difficult confession. He wasn't up to saying this to Noelle, or to anybody else for that matter, more than once.

The waitress gracefully slid their warm plates on the table in front of them. Noelle's strawberry-and-Nutella crepe. His boeuf bourguignonne. The French beef stew with its pearl onions and carrots served on a bed of whipped potatoes distracted him with its rich, wine-steeped scent. He picked up his fork before the plate was barely settled in front of him, sank it into a tender cube of beef, testing its texture, and then stopped himself. He lifted his head to apologize for his greediness but caught Noelle doing the same thing to her crepe. They shared a quick smile at their mutual hunger before taking a silently agreed-upon bite of their dinner.

The beef was perfect, the flavor of the red wine perfectly balanced in the meaty dish. He moaned with not-so-silent appreciation the same moment Noelle made a similar sound.

"This place is a keeper," she said.

"Agreed."

They both chewed in respectful and thankful silence. Then Noelle wiped her mouth with her napkin.

"You were saying…?"

Lex took a swallow of wine. What was there to say after making the statement he just had? "That's very self-explanatory."

"No, it's not. You can't say something like that and not…not explain yourself."

"I think I just did." Lex picked up his fork, but Noelle reached across the table and grabbed his plate with both hands, pulling it to her side of the table and narrowly missing knocking over the small vase of daisies.

"Nope," she said. "Explain yourself." How did she do that? Wasn't the plate too hot to touch?

Lex stared over at his plate with longing, not just for the food but for the opportunity to never have brought up the subject at all. Then, after this point, he would tell her that her sister had convinced him to date her and really end the night on a high note. He sighed.

"If I promise to tell you, will you give me back my plate?"

"How can I trust you?"

"Because I said I would." He gave her his irritated, hungry-man eyebrow.

Her eyes narrowed again. "Okay." She pushed the plate back across the table, wincing. "Damn, I swear this plate wasn't so hot the first time." She blew on her fingers while watching him across the table. "Go on. I'm waiting."

Lex considered. He could tell her some bull story about saving his sperm for the right woman…but he'd come this far. And he owed her that much plus a whole lot more. He adjusted the cloth napkin on his lap, clattered his fork at the edge of the bowl and sat back in his chair. "I've dated more than my fair share of women," he said. "It's time for me to slow down."

"Is that all there is to it?"

She *would* ask follow-up questions… "With most—all—of the women I dated recently, I slept with them too early and, because of that, the relationships ended early too. I wanted to stop having meaningless sex that didn't lead to anything."

"It's hard to make meaningless sex lead to anything but more meaningless sex and maybe a baby, if you're in the market for that sort of thing. Which I am not, by the way." She lifted her hands up like she was warning off any invading babies heading straight to her womb.

"Don't worry, I'm not looking for either one," Lex said with a laugh. He didn't examine too closely what they'd agreed to, if anything. Instead, he picked up his fork, silently asking if she was satisfied with his answer. By way of response, she shrugged and picked up her own knife and fork.

"That's actually a pretty good reason not to indulge in dirty, club sex." Noelle sliced off a piece of her crepe and put it in her mouth. She chewed slowly, watching him with an unreadable expression.

"Okay, enough with the sex talk. Let's talk about something that's the very opposite of sex."

She licked a smear of Nutella from the side of her

mouth. "I'm perfectly fine with our topic of conversation."

"Great." Because it wasn't. "We should talk about family. Family is the ultimate cold shower." Lex desperately needed that to be true. "Your sister. How's she doing?"

Lex was floundering. He wanted to talk about sex. He wanted to *have* sex. With her. But that wasn't what their dinner was about. He had an actual agenda going into this, didn't he?

Across the table, Noelle looked like someone threw a bucket of ice water in her face. "My sister? Margot?"

"Sure. Unless you have more than one."

"One is quite enough," Noelle muttered. Her utensils clattered against her plate as she abandoned them in favor of her wineglass. "What about her?"

"Is she still trying to fix your life?"

"What do you know about my sister?" Her tone was annoyed, instead of suspicious, and Lex winced at his latest misstep.

"Wasn't she trying to get you out of your so-called depression the other day? Does she still think you want to slit your wrists?"

Pursing her lips, Noelle swirled the remaining wine in her glass but didn't drink. "She's just worried about me. After our parents died, all we had left was each other. It's only natural for her to shelter her baby sister from the boogie men always waiting around the corner, even if they're in her own mind." But the way she played with her wine betrayed that wasn't all she thought about her sister's meddling ways.

Lex could tell her now. Tell her everything. He gripped the heavy silver handle of his fork, speared a slice of carrot. *Tell her.* He put the firm oval of the carrot in his mouth and slowly chewed.

"She cares about you," he said. "That's what family does. Our parents, our brothers and sisters, they do messed-up things to you out of love. Sometimes it's for your own good, sometimes it's just to prove they can control you and sometimes they act out of fear that you'll make the same mistakes they did."

"Do you think that's what Margot is doing?" she asked like he was overstepping his boundaries.

"I'm not talking about your sister," Lex said, instead of reaching for the words that were there waiting for him to speak. To tell Noelle what he'd agreed to do for Margot and then prepare himself to walk out of the restaurant and never see Noelle again.

But the words didn't come. Instead, he gave her the story of his past and what brought him to this table with her instead of a Jamaican prison.

"I was a dumb kid," he said.

Lex told her all the stupid and pointless trouble he got himself into to prove he wasn't just another Diallo heir, bloated with inherited money, who didn't have to work and could live off the family wealth if he felt like it.

From the beginning, he'd rebelled. Cherry bombing the toilets at his first private school, quickly getting himself expelled from another until his parents threw their hands up and sent him to a public school where he learned how to hack into supposedly impossible-to-crack computer systems. Weeks before his high school graduation ceremony, after years of bad behavior, he got sent to Jamaica as punishment and rehabilitation.

"But was that even a punishment, being sent off to paradise for college?"

"Oh, yes. It was definitely a punishment."

Although he was in college, his aunt and uncle, at his mother's request, had taken away everything from him except what he needed to do well in school. He was restricted to using the computer lab on campus, only had a cheap cell phone and had to come home when he wasn't in school.

Naturally, he found a way around those restrictions, signing up for a fake campus activity that explained the days and nights he danced at Margot's club.

But he didn't tell Noelle the last part.

"I hated being there, but it ended up changing my life."

If Margot hadn't sat him down and given him one of the most frightening talks of his life, he probably would have gone down a destructive path.

"It was tough love," Lex said. "But I needed it."

He shared his story, watching Noelle under the restaurant's golden light. He was stalling, taking the time to enjoy the soft glow of her and the whispered intimacy of their voices while around them the rest of the restaurant hummed with the sound of cutlery and conversation, low laughter, the unobtrusive violins coming from the speakers. He probably would never see Noelle again. This was a night he wanted to remember.

"Tough love, huh?" Noelle bit the corner of her lip. "I'm glad that worked for you, but I don't think that's what I need."

"Do you *know* what you need?"

Noelle gave a bark of unamused laughter. "For my sister to leave me alone?" She bit her lip again. "You know, when I was with you that night, that first night, I really enjoyed the time we spent together. It was like, for the first time, except for the job I have now, I had something that was all mine that Margot hadn't gotten for me or hadn't touched." She smiled at him, full and wide.

And it nearly broke him.

"All my life, my sister has been engineering my friends, my clothes, my boyfriends. Even the guy who dumped me last year was someone she arranged for me to meet. With you, it felt so good to have something apart from her. I love my sister, but she's completely taken over my life." She grimaced, a parody of a smile, admission of how doomed and hopeless it all sounded. "Our parents were careless with our lives in many ways. They left even our survival up to chance. Margot has spent her entire adult life trying to reverse the effects of that. I get it. But what she's done is just another kind of damage." Noelle took a big breath, like she was about to jump into the deep end of the pool. "Even though things might not have ended so well the other night at the club, I want to keep seeing you. I want to keep you for myself." She looked embarrassed at her admission, her eyes flickering to the table before lifting again to meet his.

Under the table, Lex clenched his fist so hard his arm trembled. "Noelle..."

She looked up at him, onyx eyes damp in the soft light, mouth still red from her lipstick, her hair a thick fall around her face and her shoulders. "Yes?"

Lex smoothed his damp palm down the cotton of his slacks, felt his thigh muscle jump with nervous energy. He opened his mouth to ruin everything between them.

But nothing came out.

Noelle looked at him in expectation, but, when he remained quiet, she took a sip from her glass of water and picked up her purse. "You know what?" Noelle opened the purse, pulled out a hundred-dollar bill and slipped it under the vase of daisies. "Let's get out of here."

Lex shook himself from the ice of indecision, removed his wallet from his back pocket and pulled out enough money to pay for the meal, mentally doing a tally in his head including tax and a generous tip. He slid the money in place of Noelle's and pushed the bill back into her hand. "I'm ready whenever you are."

For a moment, it looked like she would protest, but he stood up and gestured toward the exit, waiting for her to leave her chair. It wasn't until they were walking through the restaurant that Lex realized how long they'd been there. When they first arrived, nearly every table had been full. Now the place only had a few people still eating, the candles on the tables extinguished, leaving the tables themselves like squat shadows hugging the walls and lurking around corners, waiting for the next batch of victims, drunk on love or just the idea of romance, to walk back into their lair.

On the way out, Lex told the hostess standing bored at her station that they'd left money for the check and then he followed Noelle out into the warm night, wondering what else she had in mind for the rest of their date.

Chapter 11

The parking lot of the restaurant was nearly deserted. Only half a dozen cars, including Lex's Charger, remained and, since the restaurant had been crowded when they got there, the black sedan was a good walk away from the front door and under a sheltering of trees. Noelle walked silently at Lex's side.

Dinner hadn't gone exactly as she'd planned. Her apology went off without a hitch, but talking about family and the pain and pleasure of having people in your life who both looked out for you and hurt you, sometimes equally, had left her on the verge of tears. Noelle loved Margot, but at the best of times, her sister was too much for her to handle. Since Noelle became an adult, they'd dealt with each other best over the phone.

The car chirped and flashed its lights when Lex unlocked it.

"Home?" He asked the simple question, opening the door for her.

"Home is fine." She climbed into the car. "I'm heading out for an early brunch with Ruby and Malia tomorrow. I don't want to be too tired to enjoy them or the food."

He slid the key into the ignition but didn't turn on the engine. The car's interior lights slowly faded, leaving them enclosed in the dark. "It's all right to tell your sister you want to live your life in peace," Lex began softly, his deep voice resonant in the car's shadowed warmth. "You're both adults. I'm sure she loves you and will understand if you tell her you want to find your own lovers and your own job."

"It's not that simple," Noelle protested. Margot had been directing her life for a long time.

"It is." Lex's certainty almost made her believe it.

She drew a deep breath and incidentally pulled the scent of his cologne, of man, into her lungs. He smelled like the sea, like a hint of the stewed beef he'd eaten in the restaurant. When he spoke, a breath of the red wine they'd shared reached her nose. It made her wonder how he would taste. If it would be like their kiss at the club, all dirty intentions that called up the phantom sensation of Lex's body moving against hers, naked and sweat-slick, the thick heat of him between her legs and driving relentlessly into her. Noelle shifted her thighs under the dress, aware of the growing dampness in her panties.

He'd kissed her so well that Noelle thought she would come right there just from the hot stroke and lick of his tongue alone. If he hadn't turned her down, she was very sure they would've had sex that night. But he was celibate.

Did that mean no more kissing?

Noelle turned her head toward the open window of the car, trying to clear her nose of his intoxicating scent and pay attention to what he was saying. She cleared her throat.

"Maybe one day she and I will have that conversation," she said. "But it won't be tomorrow."

"Or even next week."

"Or even next week," she echoed, despite his obvious disappointment. Why was he so damn invested in this anyway?

But instead of being irritated by his persistence in discussing what she did or didn't do with her life, she was actually…touched. For so long, Margot had been the only one who really showed any care and tenderness for her. Even friends, as wonderful as they were, had never been concerned enough about her life to push her toward something that was a little uncomfortable but had the potential for a big payoff. His concern warmed her.

"Thank you," she said.

"For what? I haven't done anything except piss you off tonight."

"You've definitely done more than that." She leaned over the gearshift and kissed him.

Like nothing else she'd done since she lost her parents, kissing Lex was a risk. He drew in a breath against her lips, mouth burgundy-flavored, a red she tasted on his lips and wanted to lick from his tongue until she was drunk from it. She wanted this. In the club, she'd asked him to come home with her. She asked him with the proof that he wanted her pushing hard into her belly. She'd asked out loud and somehow shattered the moment between them. This time, she had no intention of asking.

He put hands on her shoulders. "Noelle."

It should have been obvious what he wanted with the way he said her name, drawing out the syllables with a sigh, but instead it was all ambiguity. Nothing like when they'd been on the boat and he was two breaths from burying himself deep inside her, with no hesitation. His reticence now forced her to be even more direct with what she wanted.

"You're gorgeous," she said and kissed him more deeply as she climbed to her knees in the seat, leaning into him to clasp his face between her hands and lick along his mouth, tonguing her way inside to taste his teeth, the soft flesh behind his lips. He breathed out her name and she smiled against his mouth, nibbled on the plump pink of his bottom lip and sucked it in her mouth.

He made a noise, hot and urgent with want, but he didn't touch her. If anything, he sank deeper into his seat. The leather moaned and exhaled its particular scent, and, beneath that, she smelled him too. Masculine and almost too warm, an insistent heat she wanted at the back of her throat. Noelle scraped a hand along his jaw, teasing at the faint stubble that pricked her fingers, one by one. The sound of the rough hairs against her fingertips, loud in the locked and airless car, sparked goose bumps along her body. He flinched into her touch and opened his mouth for her.

"Noelle…" He moaned her name, no ambiguity this

time, the breath hitching at the back of his throat like a sob.

She opened her mouth over his and swallowed her name. Want snapped in her belly when a wordless sound vibrated between them. She pressed closer and felt his arms, long and locked and straining, fingers hinged tight to the edges of his seat, squeaking against the leather, as if that grip alone would save him from the conflagration Noelle already felt rising between them. She climbed into his lap, hiking up her skirt to flirt at the tops of her thighs, and she felt him groan again.

He was hard for her. She pressed down into him and he bucked up into her. "Yeah?"

"Noelle...?" He pressed her name between his teeth until the syllables sounded like pain, but when he grabbed her thighs to keep her pressing down on him, she knew she'd won whatever battle was raging between her and his celibacy. Noelle reached back, unzipped her dress and the thin cotton tumbled down around her shoulders, around her waist. In the darkness of the car, with only the light from the parking lot to illuminate what they were doing, he was fierce and shadowed, his eyes flicking down to her suddenly naked breasts. He licked his lips, gripped her thighs hard enough to bruise. But, other than that, he did nothing. Noelle smiled. Then she licked her thumbs, one after the other, rubbed the new wetness there across her already hard nipples. Once. Twice. Moaned at how good it felt with his breath huffing against her skin. Lex licked his lips again, obviously hungry for what she had, so she fed him. Took a breast in hand and, with her thumb under her nipple, put it in his mouth.

He opened his mouth, breath gusting with a sigh over her skin, lips latching onto her nipple with masculine greed. He sucked and she whimpered at the sensation that uncurled between her legs.

He moaned into her skin, reached up almost tentatively to touch the other breast. But once it was under his hand, he plucked her nipple, flicked it, humming with pleasure as she snaked in his lap and slowly went out of her mind from just his mouth alone. Her panties were soaked and the desperate scent of her was hot in the car. The power had shifted. A butterfly touch stroked her panty line, and it was her turn to gasp a little louder. His touch became firmer, curving under the fabric to feel her. She groaned as his fingers slid in her wetness, stroked a moan from her lips and then stuttering versions of his name.

Lex's mouth left her breast with a soft pop and his shadowed eyes rose to hers. "Backseat," he growled.

She wasted no time getting there, scrambling off his lap and moving to the wider space without an ounce of shame, although she felt the relatively cool air on her bare bottom and on the sliver of her sex Lex had exposed when he pulled her panties to the side. Between settling herself behind tinted windows and wishing Lex would hurry, she felt him behind her, lying on his back on the long seat and pushing her forward, until her forehead bumped almost tenderly into the glass. Noelle shivered at the metallic sound of his belt buckle being undone and then his zipper. A gentle hand snaked around her belly and pulled her slowly and backward up his body over the fabric of his slacks, his bare and furred thighs, the jut of his hips and...

"I've wanted you for so long." He groaned into the

back of her neck as he fingered aside her panties again. "So damn long."

Another part of him, latex-covered and much bigger, nudged at her wetness, stroked over her before sliding deeply and firmly home. Noelle clenched around him, wet and urgent, the pleasure from just having him inside her enough to make her moan his name. Her breath stuttered in her throat when he slid a hand in her panties to stroke her clit. Fingers tugged at her nipples one after the other and she felt her entire world begin to rock with the first movements of Lex's hips.

It was the first time that night but not the last.

Chapter 12

At dance class the next day, she was sore. And Ruby did not miss it. During their first break, she practically pounced on Noelle.

"He left you walking funny, huh?"

From her seat on the low bench near the studio's open window, Noelle groaned silently behind the towel hiding her face. With the excuse of wiping the sweat from her brow and neck, she hid her hot cheeks before she looked at Ruby.

"Why do you always mess with me?"

"I'm thinking that's a *yes*." Ruby's gaze was wicked and pleased and she inspected Noelle from the top of her ponytailed head to the New Balance sneakers on her feet. "I bet he knocked it right out of the park."

"What are you guys talking about?" Malia emerged from a group of dancers nearby, which included a new guy who looked, according to her, like the Italian ballet dancer Roberto Bolle, especially when he wore his sweats real tight. Ruby gave Noelle a smiling glance but didn't say anything about what she'd guessed, sexual bloodhound that she was. Despite her freedom with sex, she wasn't one to tell someone else's business.

"Nothing interesting," Noelle muttered. She folded her towel over her thigh. "I went out with Lex last night and—"

"Rode him like a racehorse?" Malia asked with a dirty smile.

"Um... I wouldn't say that, but we did have fun together." She adjusted and readjusted her ponytail, desperately needing something to do with her hands while the two women looked at her like she'd just confessed to winning a million-dollar jackpot.

"Wow..." Malia sat on the floor near Noelle's feet. "Was he amazing in the sack?"

Ruby leaned closer to hear the answer while Noelle glanced quickly around the room, making sure their conversation was private. Milton held court near the stereo controls, surrounded by most of the people in the class and dispensing witticisms and praise like candy. Nobody was really paying attention to them.

"I am not going to talk about him like that." Noelle shook her head, but she couldn't stop a smile from bursting through.

"Oh!" Ruby breathed and dropped down beside Malia. "He must be a god between the sheets. I don't think I've ever seen you smile like that, like *ever*."

"I smile plenty, thank you very much."

"Smile, yes. Big and wide like this, hell no." Ruby looped an arm around Noelle's shoulders, her expression turning serious. "And that's okay. It's good to start healing from old trauma and creating new pleasures and memories."

"Yeah…" Malia touched her knee. "The good thing about pain is that it eventually fades away."

Across the room, Milton clapped his hands, attracting the class's attention. "Okay, everyone. Let's get back to our places and hit this routine one more time."

Malia got to her feet. "I want to hear more about this delicious and happy event," she said.

"Yes." Ruby stood up and adjusted the headband around her short hair. "Let's go to that juice bar we were talking the other day."

Although Noelle was a little shy about the idea of sharing details of what she and Lex had done, or even about what they meant to each other, she could use a quick outing with the girls. Their raunchiness and unconditional acceptance kept her sane. A good balance to her own uncertainty about where she and Lex stood. The sex had been amazing, the most satisfying she'd ever had. And despite her suspicion that their night together meant little to Lex, she wanted more.

"The juice bar sounds good."

But at the end of class, Noelle checked her messages while waiting for the girls to finish up in the locker room and saw that she had a voice mail and text from her sister.

Am I picking you up or do you want to meet there?

She frowned at the message just as a reminder popped up at the top of the phone.

Art by Night with Margot.

Damn. She'd promised her sister she'd go on the art walk without even looking at her calendar. She cursed again.

Ruby came out of the locker room with jokes. "What's got you looking so much like your sister?"

Noelle politely gave her the finger.

Ruby grinned. "I doubt you even know what to do with that finger." But she quickly lost the smile. "Seriously though, what's wrong?"

"I forgot I agreed to go to this art thing with Margot." The last thing she wanted to do was see Margot, especially after the intense discussion she and Lex had gotten into about her the other night.

Malia walked up behind Ruby. "Does that mean you're ditching us?"

"I wouldn't say it like that. My phone just reminded me about it."

"I don't think your phone likes us very much." Malia pouted.

"It's cool, honey." Ruby gave her arm a reassuring squeeze. "Go and have family time. Malia and I will talk a bunch of mess about you while we sip our healthy smoothies."

Noelle rolled her eyes but grabbed Ruby in a tight hug, grateful for her understanding. "I'll make it up to you guys after next class. My treat."

"There's nothing to make up for. Go! And make sure to tell us what fancy place your sister takes you for dinner and how much everything cost."

Laughing, Noelle slung her duffel bag over her shoulder, gave the two women quick hugs and took off. She had just enough time to rush home, take a proper shower and change into something suitable. Even though it was the annual Art by Night—a weekend event similar to Nuit Blanche in Paris and a few other countries—she had the feeling her sister was going to dress up, maybe even have her come along as a plus one at an exclusive party or three.

After driving only ten miles above the speed limit on surface streets, she was only fifteen minutes late getting to Miami Beach. Noelle climbed out of her car near a Ferris wheel lit up with white halogen lights just for the weekend. The streets streamed with people ready to see the expensive and beautiful art installations in celebration of what Margot called "an elevated Miami." Artists from all over the world arrived in the city to go to the giant art party. Noelle had only been to Art by Night a few times but never had access to the private parties like her sister. She found Margot near the steep steps of her favorite museum. The steps had been transformed into a neon keyboard and played a note of piano music whenever someone stepped on it.

"Hey."

Margot stood apart from the swirling crowd of mostly adults running up and down the steps and laughing in delight at the notes their feet played. The lights from the steps glowed behind her, outlining her elegant silhouette and bright green shoes. She looked beautiful and untouchable.

"You look good," Margot said, smiling, the look of approval glowing in her eyes.

"Thanks."

Noelle was glad she'd made the effort and changed into the black Helmut Lang sheath dress she'd splurged on a few months before. Pairing the dress with her most comfortable high heels, also black, she was fairly certain she wouldn't embarrass her sister wherever they ended up that night.

"You ready?" she asked.

"Yep."

Noelle walked at her sister's side, weaving through the crowd that moved steadily through the street, which was blocked off to vehicular traffic. The palm trees on Collins glowed in rainbow colors, wrapped in coils of light. A small crowd followed a performer balanced on ten-foot-high stilts and trailing rainbow confetti on outstretched arms. Music floated through the streets, one of the Gipsy Kings songs Noelle had been obsessed with in college.

The music was infectious and Noelle smiled, shimmying her hips to the beat with each step. Maybe she'd suggest a salsa dance number to Milton the next class.

"I was on my way here when it occurred to me that you might forget we were meeting up," Margot said.

Noelle's smile died. "I actually did forget. But I'm here."

"I hope you weren't too far away."

Was that her not-so-subtle way of trying to find out what Noelle was doing when she got the reminder text?

"I wasn't too far, only up in North Beach, but I had to go home and change."

"Your therapist's office?" The look on Margot's face was deliberately unconcerned, but Noelle wasn't fooled. She never told Margot she was seeing a therapist and she certainly never let her know which one.

"No. That's not where I was." She didn't want to be a bitch about it, she really didn't. But did every younger sister have to put up with this kind of stalking from their sibling?

Noelle blew out a quiet breath of frustration and tried to calm herself down. The Gipsy Kings song faded away and Ottmar Liebert's lively guitar took its place.

Margot pointed with the rolled-up program for Art by Night. "The first installation is that way."

They followed the trailing group across the brightly lit sidewalk and up the steps into a high-rise hotel with a beautiful Art Deco facade. White marble everywhere, echoing footsteps, soft violin music in the lobby. A woman dressed as a harlequin, her painted smile a little maniacal, guided them toward a black spiral staircase.

"It's on the top floor," Margot said with a look at her stilettos. "Let's take the elevator instead."

In the glass elevator, it was just the two of them. The car slowly rose toward the sky in a whisper of sound, the floor shuddering minutely under Noelle's feet. She stood on one side of car, thoughts and indecisions floating through her mind but not to her mouth. Margot stood with her purse clasped in her hands and held against her thighs. She seemed deep in thought, her gaze trained on a spot to the right of Noelle's head. The car came to a stop and the door slid open.

Noelle stepped out of the car and into another world. "I'm not a child anymore, Margot."

Roars, deep-throated and long, met them as they left the elevator. More sounds, high shrieks like Noelle had heard in dinosaur movies and documentaries. She and Margot stood under a high, glassed-in roof, an empty loft space with dozens of people and room enough for dozens more.

The roof was twenty feet or so above them. But instead of looking out to the dark, starry sky, the glass had been strung with fine lines of light woven together to sketch a skyscape of dragons. The roof was the only source of light in the room.

Gasps of excitement drifted around the room, breaking through the dragon roars and screeches. It was all very impressive. Noelle walked along a far wall, watching the story unfolding above her of the dragon being born from an egg, small and delicate. In the next panel it was larger but still a graceful and unthreatening shape against the night sky. By the last panel, the dragon was large enough to stretch from wall to wall. Wings spread, fire breathing, tail curled.

"Beautiful," Margot said.

"Yes." Noelle traced its shape with her eyes. "I wonder if it scares the smaller dragons."

"No. It shouldn't. It's older, but they're still the same kind."

Noelle looked at Margot. "But does the bigger dragon remember what it's like to be small? Does it know they are the same?"

They weren't talking about the exhibit anymore.

"Is that how you see me?" Margot asked.

"Isn't that how you see yourself?"

The noise of the other people in the room buffeted Noelle, coming at her from all sides—people talking about the exhibit, wondering out loud what happened to the dragon's genitals.

"Can we…can we get out of here?"

Margot looked briefly around them, a vigilant glance that surprised Noelle. Was she annoyed about possibly leaving the show?

"Of course we can. Let's go."

They took the elevator down, but this time they had plenty of company, the car full enough to push Noelle into the back of the car with Margot and to force the smell of different colognes and perfumes into her nose. When the elevator stopped, she gently pushed her way out and dragged in a lungful of artificially cold air.

Margot took her to a coffee shop a few blocks away. It was full of the obviously Art by Night crowd—some in cocktail dresses, hipster beards and self-consciously artsy T-shirts—curving in a long line from the front register. But most were getting their drinks to go. More than half of the cafe's fifteen or so tables were empty. They found a table and sat down. A girl behind the counter gave them the stink eye, probably for not buying something before sitting down. Noelle and Margot both ignored her.

"You want something?" Margot asked.

"Yeah, but I'll wait until the line is a little shorter." Noelle waved at the line that was actually getting longer. "This is ridiculous."

She leaned into the wooden back of her chair and dropped her purse on the table. She felt suddenly very, very tired.

"What's on your mind, Noelle?"

She wasn't quick enough to stop a sigh from escaping. "A lot of things."

Margot crossed her legs and waited. She looked ready to wait for as long as it took, settling back into her chair and curving her hands around her small handbag. It was an expression Noelle was very familiar with from her youthful days of pouting about something she wasn't ready to talk about until hours later.

"I don't want to be a lawyer."

Margot's eyebrow inched up, but she didn't say anything. She was still waiting.

"I don't want you to stalk me to my shrink's office. I don't want you to introduce me to any more men. I don't want you to keep treating me like a child." She pressed her lips together. "Or a prisoner."

Although she didn't move, didn't make a sound, Noelle felt Margot's sudden tension, a tightening of her whole body. Noelle curled her fingers into her palms, her mouth open to instantly apologize for what she'd said, but she stopped herself just in time. Her hands were sweating. She felt so…ungrateful. But she wanted her freedom too.

Finally, Margot spoke. "Is that how you feel? Like a prisoner?"

"Sometimes, yeah. I mean, how else do you expect me to feel when I find out you had someone follow me to my therapist's office." Margot must have hired another person to do the work. She couldn't imagine her sister lurking outside her doctor's door in her tailored Armani suit and Manolo Blahniks.

"You're being…" She stopped and took a breath. "I just want you to be safe, Noelle."

"I am safe. What's going to happen to me in my little paralegal office or even at my therapist's? My life is pretty boring, Margot. I go to work, I go home, I go out with friends a couple of nights a week and I see you. It's the very boring life of a typical twenty-six-year-old. You have to remember what that's like."

The corner of Margot's mouth pulled up. "That was never the life I had at twenty-six."

Of course it wasn't. Noelle swallowed hard and fiddled with the zipper of her purse. Sometimes it was all too easy to forget that Margot never had the luxury of a normal *anything*. Their parents disappeared her first year of college, forcing her to suddenly have the complete responsibility of caring for a nine-year-old. She had dropped out of college and gone from being Noelle's older sister, always there when their parents disappeared on one of their alcohol-fueled binges, to the stern parental figure who helped with homework, who made sure they had someplace to sleep and food to eat, and who stopped smiling.

"I do remember that, Margot. Sometimes I forget, but it's not because I'm ungrateful. Because I know I couldn't have made it this far without you giving up so much." The guilt twisted in her stomach. "I just… I just don't want to feel I have to live my life the way you want me to just because you saved me."

An emotion twisted Margot's mouth and she looked almost angry. "I never wanted that from you." A tear slid down her face in a quick rush, like it was trying to hide itself. Margot dashed it away with a quick finger. "You don't owe me anything." She cursed, darted a look toward the front counter where the line had actually gotten shorter. "Excuse me a second."

With her head low and turned away from Noelle, she left the table and joined the line at the front of the café.

By the time Margot made it back with a cup of green tea for Noelle and black coffee for herself, she had herself under control again. Her face was dry and her makeup was flawless. She put the tea in front of Noelle and took a sip from the insulated paper cup that already had a smear of her burgundy lipstick on its edge. She sat down like she was facing an executioner.

"Is that why you've been down the last few months? Because of me keeping you prisoner?"

"Not completely, but yes."

She could feel the shift across the table, the same one she could feel inside herself, of Margot falling into the pit of the past, remembering all the ways their parents had failed them. "All I want to do is live my own life," Noelle finished.

For the first time ever, Noelle saw a look of embarrassment on her sister's face. "Someone said that to me the other day. They said that you're fine and not as broken and in need of fixing as I think."

"You're telling strangers about my private business now?" Noelle plucked at the sleeve around her to-go teacup.

"No, no. It's nothing like that. It's somebody you know."

"Really? Who?"

Margot waved a hand in dismissal. "No one we have to discuss right now." She sipped her coffee, methodically putting her painted mouth on the edge of the rim that was already smeared with lipstick. "I'm…sorry about trying to force a different life on you. I really am. I…" She popped the top of the coffee cup on and then off again. "Our parents forced this life on me." Noelle flinched and drew her hand away from the center of the table, but Margot grabbed it. "I did it to take care of both of us, not just you, so don't start making that face." She squeezed Noelle's hand so hard that it hurt. "I would've never chosen this kind of life for myself. I'm always working, and I know too much about human nature to ever trust anyone. So I'm just saying, finally, that I understand what you've been trying to tell me all this time. Okay?"

Noelle squeezed back and then slowly withdrew her hand with a wince. Margot looked ready to apologize, but Noelle replaced her hand on top of her sister's. "Okay."

The smile they shared felt like the first real one between them in years.

By the time they finished their drinks, Margot was sagging in her chair and looked absolutely drained.

"Are you okay?"

"I am." Margot picked up her empty coffee cup. "But I think I'm ready to call it a night."

"All right. Let's go." Noelle took the cup from Margot and tossed it in the trash with her own. They left the coffee shop just as another big group from Art by Night flooded in. She walked Margot to her car, a slow and mostly silent journey with her sister's arm around her waist. At the car, Margot held her in a long hug.

"Text me when you get home," Noelle said.

"Shouldn't I be the one saying that to you?"

"We can both look out for each other." She squeezed Margot's waist. "So you text me when you get home, and I'll do it too."

Margot's smile had a touch of sadness at the edges, a wistfulness. "Okay. I'll text you and we'll talk tomorrow."

Noelle watched the black Benz drive off with a sense of lightness, the pressure she'd been feeling more and more lately floating off her chest. She smiled to herself. Why had it taken so long for her to tell her sister what she was feeling? If it hadn't been for Lex encouraging her to spill her truth, she would have carried so much unnecessary weight around on her shoulders for who knows how long. She took a deep breath.

On a whim, she pulled out her phone and texted Lex.

I talked to my sister about what you said. So much better. She promises a complete 180.

She hesitated before pressing Send, not sure if they even knew each other well enough to exchange texts that had nothing to do with sex or meeting up for drinks. But less than a minute after she sent the text, his response buzzed in her palm.

Good. Talking is actually good for more than just fore-play.

Noelle huffed a soft laugh into the backs of her fingers. Just then, another message came through.

Lex: I want to see you. Can I come over later?

I'm actually out. At Art by Night.

Lex: Miami Beach? Meet me in ten. I'm nearby.

Noelle hesitated. Was this a booty call at a nearby hotel? From the one and only time they'd slept together, she knew he lived in Little Haiti. That was about ten miles away.

Lex: I'm at Bello e Bello Pizza on Collins. Come keep me company until more foreplay?

Yes, yes, yes. Her body answered before her fingers even lifted to type a reply. She made herself sound less desperate though, agreeing to meet him in fifteen minutes which was plenty of time to get through the Art by Night traffic.

A little over ten minutes later, she walked up to the late-night pizza place that served the best Chicago-style slices in Miami. Lex didn't see her, but she saw him sitting with four other people at an outdoor table, his legs sprawled in jeans, a plain white T-shirt draped over his wide chest, nodding in agreement as he listened to whatever it was that another man was saying. He looked so serious, so relaxed. So beautiful.

Her high heels clicked across the sidewalk, keeping time with her heart's anticipatory beat. Even though it had been less than a day since she had left his bed, she missed him. She allowed herself to feel that eagerness, to want him, not just his touch or his kisses but all parts of him in her life.

A shiver ran through her. Doubt and excitement both. She must have done something to alert him because suddenly he looked up and a full-on smile took over his face. An army of butterflies invaded her stomach. And she felt an answering grin shape her lips.

"Hey."

"Hey, yourself."

Damn. He was gorgeous.

His smile widened like he knew what she was thinking and highly approved.

"Are you two just going to stare at each other all night?"

Noelle blinked and looked away from Lex. "I'm

sorry. Hi." She gave the four other people at the table her best smile.

"Everyone, this is Noelle," Lex said and pulled her into his lap. He nuzzled her neck, filling her senses with the crisp smell of his aftershave, slightly worn from the long evening, along a hint of tomato sauce on his breath. For a brief moment, she wallowed in the luxury of him, his chest, his smell, his smile like the sunrise, before she raised her eyes to look again at the others sitting at the table with him. She drew a sharp breath.

All four, including his twin whom she'd already met, looked like him. Smooth skin, sleek bodies and gorgeous enough to be on the covers of international magazines. Lex had invited her out to meet his brothers and sisters. At least some of them.

They each introduced themselves (Taj, Temple, Alice and, of course, Adisa) and then went back to what they had been discussing—how safe it was for someone named Elia to travel alone in Thailand—while Lex rocked his legs beneath her.

"I'm glad you could come," he rumbled, looking up at her with eyes that made her feel like the most desirable woman in the world.

"Are you sure it's okay?" She darted a look at his siblings. "We're the only ones…you know." She gestured to their close bodies, self-conscious but also content to stay balanced on his knee and absorbing his warmth.

"We're fine," Alice spoke up. "As long as you don't start swapping spit in front of us, we'll cope." She flashed Noelle another smile and poked one of the twin brothers, Temple. "I want something sweet. Come with me and help me decide."

The two siblings wandered into the pizza parlor, already debating sweet crepe versus chocolate cake. Which was no contest as far as Noelle was concerned. Crepes every time.

"This is the first time you've brought a girl around," Adisa spoke to her brother over Noelle's head.

Lex only hummed a dismissal in response.

Taj snickered. "How is that celibacy thing going?"

Lex gave him the finger and Noelle pressed her burning cheeks into her palms.

Is this what she missed out on by not having siblings her age?

Adisa laughed but not unkindly. "Ignore us. We're just teasing."

"I figured as much. I'm just not—"

A screech cut her off just as a clatter of high heels stopped at their table. Three women stood entirely too close, all skinny with wealth dripping from their throats and wrists despite their tacky Swarovski crystal–studded dresses.

"Oh my God! I told her it was you." The three were all obviously drunk and reminded Noelle of the woman who'd dropped into Lex's lap on the boat weeks before.

One of them pointed at Lex. "You're Alexander the Great Snake, aren't you?"

A hush fell over the table and then there was a masculine snicker.

Noelle looked around the table in confusion. Adisa looked annoyed and Taj laughed again.

"Not this again," Adisa muttered. "I thought we were done."

Done with what?

Noelle felt like she was on the outside of the joke. Or whatever it was, since, judging by Lex's face, it was far from funny. She tightened her hold on his arm.

"It's been a few years, but you're still sexy as hell." The woman who'd pointed dropped into an almost conversational tone, her screeching finished, and moved closer to Lex.

Noelle slipped from his lap and stood up, her hand on his shoulder. He was as tense as steel under her touch. "Maybe you should take your party someplace else," she said.

"What? It's not every day you run into the best stripper you've ever seen in your life." The woman looked at Noelle. "I bet you've seen him in action. Even without all the muscle he had before, he's still gorgeous."

"Oh my God! I remember him. Can he dance for us right now?" The one in pink turned to Lex, tottering and drunkenly hopeful. "Dance for us!" But Lex only watched her, still sprawled in his seat, looking completely at ease. Only because her hand was touching his rigid shoulder did Noelle know differently. Lex shook his head at the woman but didn't say anything.

"Okay, ladies." Taj joined Noelle at Lex's side. "Just let the man enjoy the night in peace."

Once he spoke, the women started to size him up too. Their eyes moving hungrily over him like they pictured him naked and hanging from a pole just for them.

"Are you—?"

"Don't let things get ugly," Noelle snapped, suddenly impatient with the whole thing. "You're interrupting our evening. I'm sure you can find something better to do down the road." She jerked her head to the sidewalk.

"Oh I get it, you have a woman now. True. We all have to change when we boo up." She sighed, eyes misty like she was watching a Lifetime movie, beautiful and tragic. "Have a great night." the woman said and then snagged her arms around the waists of the other two. "Come on, girls. Let's get a cab to King of Diamonds. I'm in the mood to see some hot people dancing to trap music."

The women clattered off on their high heels, remarkably steady as they wove through the thick Collins Avenue pedestrian traffic. Under her hand, Lex's shoulder remained tense.

"What was that about?" Noelle looked down at him and then at his siblings.

"Just some annoying drunk chicks," Adisa said at the same time Taj said something Noelle didn't hear.

"Ghosts from the past," Lex finally said. He rolled his shoulders and, even though the careless expression was still on his face, she could feel even more tension radiate from him.

Alice and Temple walked out of the pizza parlor, both carrying half a crepe. "What did we miss?"

"Some women who saw Lex dance in Jamaica a million years ago and are still wetting their panties." Adisa stood up. "You all ready to go?"

Alice scrunched up her face. "We just got our sweet things."

"You can eat and walk." Adisa grabbed her sister's elbow. "Come on, guys."

Taj threw a sympathetic glance at Lex and stood up

with a scrape of the metal chair against the concrete sidewalk. "Later, brother."

The Diallos trailed away from the pizza parlor, strains of their conversation floating on the wind back to Noelle.

"Why did we have to leave? I wasn't ready."

"Lex should come with us…"

The table felt empty without them, the chairs left at angles to the table and littered with crumbs and wrinkled napkins. Noelle sank into one of the empty chairs, pressed her knees together and looked at Lex.

"You were a stripper?"

The second the words left her mouth, she felt like an idiot and a prude. Two things she'd never once associated with herself.

Before she could apologize and ask in a different way, Lex swiped a hand over his face and blew out a breath. "Yeah. When I was in college, I did dance." Now that the strange women and his siblings were gone, he seemed to settle into a different version of himself, slightly nervous. Hard-jawed. Like he was bracing himself for something.

"In Jamaica?"

"Yes."

"That's not…that's not a big deal," she said carefully. "Why didn't you tell me before? We've talked about everything else." Dread, a cold and heavy weight, dropped into Noelle's stomach. If he'd hidden such a simple thing from her, what else was he not telling her?

"It was a long time ago and I don't talk about it." He didn't say it didn't matter. "The stripping and other things I got up to back then are things I prefer to keep in the past, like teenage acne or an addiction to porn."

She jerked her gaze to his face. "You were a porn addict?"

He laughed, a painful sound. "No." His fingers tapped a disjointed rhythm across the chrome surface of the table. "Sorry. Bad joke."

His eyebrows jerked once and he looked at a point over her head. "That part of me is in the past and, although while I was doing it I wasn't ashamed, these days I don't want my parents to know what I did just because I was bored."

Noelle knew what it was like to be half caught between the past and the present. It had taken her years to be able to talk about her parents' drug and alcohol addiction to anyone but Margot and even longer to trust herself with a drink out of fear she would become like her mother. The things Lex revealed were nothing in the larger scheme of things, the bad decisions of a boy who'd had nothing to rebel against but the privileges and safety he was born with.

But he'd lied to her. It was something small, but she couldn't ignore it.

The night in the reggae club, she had asked a simple question: *Where'd you learn to dance?*

By watching you, he'd said, whispering the lie against her lips.

She pressed her purse against her stomach, nearly sick with the uncertainty that cut through the elation she'd felt being with Lex and his siblings.

"I have to go," she said.

"Noelle..." He stood up the same time she did, his chair screeching back from the table. "Stay." He cupped her elbow, tugging her closer to his warmth and the desperation in his eyes. "I'll tell you everything you want to know."

She felt herself weakening, the hardness of her suspicions melting with his touch and the naked emotion on his face. But she couldn't afford to ignore her gut instinct telling her there was something else lurking behind his lie. She needed time and space to think. "I can't. I know this shouldn't be a big deal, but... I can't stop thinking about what this could mean."

"Like what?" He asked the question, but she could see the flicker of something—an awareness—at the back of his eyes.

Noelle pulled back until his hand fell away from her elbow and the feel of it was like a tightly pulled string about to snap in two. "I can't do this now. I'm sorry."

She turned away from the devastation in his face and left Collins Avenue with her heart beating fast and painful in her throat. Instead of heading home, she found herself driving the path to Margot's condo. At each turn on the side streets, she made an effort to see logic and not damn Lex with the memory of her past experiences. But all she could remember was the lie.

At Margot's downtown Miami condo, she flashed her ID to the doorman and used her key to get into the penthouse elevator. She called Margot on the way up.

"Hey," she said once her sister answered the phone. "Are you still up?"

"Of course." But the rustling of cloth, like sheets on a bed, came through the phone and made Noelle feel selfish. Maybe she should have just gone home. It was a long time past midnight.

"I can come back some other time," she said.

More rustling, the sound of glass on glass like she

was putting something down on that ridiculously expensive coffee table of hers. "Stop your foolishness. Come on up."

Margot's front door was open by the time she got there, a welcome spill of light inviting her into her sister's glassed-in loft. It was an odd place. Floor-to-ceiling windows, glass fixtures and furniture. The only things not hard and reflective were the leather pieces in the room. Black sofa, armchair and dining room furniture visible from the living room.

"Come in." Margot stood by the sofa, folding a blanket. She draped it over the back of the leather sofa and reached out to pull Noelle into a stiff hug. "Are you okay?" Her sister blinked, drowsy-looking and slow. The leggings and oversized T-shirt she wore made her look soft and inviting, not at all like someone who lived in such a cold place.

"Um…maybe."

Margot guided her to the sofa and went into the kitchen where Noelle heard the high-pitched whistle of the tea kettle. Moments later, she was back with two cups of mint tea, a jar of honey and cubes of brown sugar balanced on a silver tray. She sat close to Noelle and prepared tea for them both.

"Tell me what's wrong." She pressed the warm teacup into Noelle's cold hands.

A shiver worked its way from Noelle's scalp to her toes. She didn't want to be weak like this. Hadn't she just insisted to Margot that she was a grown-up now and didn't need any more mothering?

But she was tired of holding this thing, whatever it was, within herself.

"The guy I'm dating is lying to me." She blurted

out the words and waited for Margot to say something, to offer to make a call initiating a full background check, to ask Noelle if she was sure. But in the resulting silence, she stared into the depths of her teacup. Tiny green leaves floated in the water and sugar mixture, unmoored things plucked and isolated from far-off bushes. "You know Lex, don't you?"

Nearly an hour after it happened, the moment of the women's approach up to the table on Collins Avenue still felt surreal. After sleeping with Lex and allowing her feelings for him to bubble up and fizz inside her, a celebration of the journey to self-acceptance she was well on the way to, everything seemed suspect.

Margot had traveled to Jamaica a lot while Noelle had been in school. Her sister made sure to leave only when Noelle was away at summer camp or any of the academies where there were other adults to supervise her teenage behavior. Those women on Collins Avenue acted like anyone in Jamaica at the same time as Lex would know him. Alexander the Great Snake.

Damn. What a name.

"What's going on, Noelle?"

She'd been so deeply buried in her thoughts she didn't notice that Margot was farther away from her on the couch than when they'd sat down. She noticed now though. And also noticed the slight wrinkle between her sister's otherwise smooth brows. Sometimes she wondered if Margot had had surgery or if her skin was so flawless simply because she rarely smiled.

"The man I've been seeing. Lex. Did you ever get a lap dance from him? Did he blow your mind so much that you have dreams about him ten years later."

"Noelle, Alexander is a child to me."

Margot's words hammered into her brain and left a dizzying echo that made Noelle swallow and swallow again before she could talk. "He's a child?"

"Of course. He could be my baby brother. I wouldn't have let him dance for me, much less sleep with me." Whatever impression of softness Noelle had had about Margot was completely gone. The bones of her face stood out in severe relief against her skin. The look in her eyes was sharp enough to cut.

Margot's words washed over Noelle, but she wasn't sure she was hearing them right. Her sister actually did *know* Lex. Had known him in Jamaica. Knew his full name.

"Margot, how…?" But she couldn't go on.

"So he told you?" Margot's question was one she wasn't quite sure how to answer except with the truth.

"Yes, he did." Noelle fumbled to bring the teacup to her mouth but dropped her hand at the last minute. She didn't trust herself not to shake and spill tea all over her dress. Something was snaking in the air between them, a truth she could feel but couldn't see yet. As if her mouth was separate from her thoughts, it opened and kept talking. "At first, I couldn't believe it. But sometimes the truth is unbelievable, right?" Lex. A dancer. Margot. Who had known him then and never told Noelle.

"He wasn't supposed to tell you," Margot said. Emotion rippled over her face, transforming her beauty into something desperate and seeking. "I know you're upset, but I only did it because I was worried about you."

"Margot, you did…" *What does his past have to do with you?* She blinked at her sister, a pulse of worry beginning to pound in her throat.

But her body knew something before her mind did and her hands began a more intense tremor that rocked the teacup against the saucer, a frantic tapping that charted her rising agitation. She shoved the cup and saucer on the coffee table and squeezed her hands tight in her lap. Another truth slithering out to bite her.

"I didn't know if you were okay after Eric left," Margot said. "I just thought if Lex went out with you a few times, you would forget about Eric and start being happy again. He was only supposed to help you past the hump and get you out of your depression."

Past the hump? Depression?

The words tumbled over Noelle like lead bricks, one after the other until she was dizzy and dumb from shock. She opened her mouth a few times, cleared her throat before she was finally able to say anything. "Did…did you pay him to sleep with me too?"

"You slept with him?" The emotion on her sister's face was unmistakably anger then. Dimly Noelle thought she should be grateful for small mercies. She stumbled to her feet, face hot as she turned in a frantic circle, her hands gripped tight against her belly.

"You paid Lex to date me." It sounded too ridiculous.

"I never paid," Margot said with a hard shake of her head. She watched Noelle with a mounting fear so obvious that it was frightening. "He did it for me as a favor."

Noelle's stomach clenched and a wrecked sound left her throat. Her entire body flushed with anger. "You told him—he's one of yours? He's always been one of yours?"

And the things she'd said to Lex came back to her in nauseating detail. Her confession to him in the restaurant, the things she said when they rocked together, locked in heat in his car. The things she felt for him.

"He's yours." No longer a question.

Margot stood up, frowning. "I thought you already knew." Her face stretching in a look of deeper horror.

Noelle's disbelief and anger spilled out in a bitter splash of vomit all over Margot's carpet, over her shoes. She couldn't control it. Her face felt hot. A scorching line of tears. Throat raw.

Margot grabbed the blanket from the couch and came toward Noelle with it spread out, but Noelle backed away from her. "You did this to me." She swallowed until the unwanted moisture drained away from the bed of her tongue, the sickness receding, and she could stand without stooping over. "I thought you loved me." Noelle didn't wait for what her sister was going to say. She ran from the living room, from the condo. At the elevator, she frantically pressed the button for it to come, panting and shivering.

This can't be happening.

"Noelle, please! Come and let me explain." Margot ran after her, feet bare, the sleeve of her oversized shirt falling down her shoulder.

"No! Stay away from me!" Noelle ran for the stairs.

Noelle ran until her lungs burned, racing down flight after flight of stairs until she was sure Margot wasn't behind her. Then she stopped on a lower floor and took the elevator the rest of the way down. In the lobby, she hid her tear-streaked face from the guard and ran out to the sidewalk, craning her head looking desperately for a cab. But none appeared. The idea of standing outside her sister's condo, on her street, made sickness rise up in her again, sharp and urgent. She pressed a fist into her stomach then and, after barely thinking about another option, started walking toward her house. Without her purse or her car keys. Without any idea how she would make it all the way there.

Chapter 13

Lex opened his door at nearly three in the morning to see Noelle's ravaged face staring back at him.

She was barefoot and carrying her high heels in one hand and wore dried tears streaked over her face like war paint. But she seemed almost calm.

Fear kicked in his chest and his hand tightened around the doorknob. "It's late," Lex said, low and gentle like talking to a feral animal on the verge of trusting him. "Come inside."

At first, she didn't react to him. Her face stayed blank. Only her eyes moved over him, eager and hard, hungry and hurt. Then her entire body heaved with a breath and she blinked rapidly, Sleeping Beauty waking.

"I really liked you, Lex." The words left Noelle's mouth on a wisp of breath, just loud enough for him to hear even though he had to lean close. "You screwing me over is almost okay, but I can't believe my own sister, who I actually…love and who I thought loved me too, did this to me." Noelle slammed a closed fist into her chest and the sound was loud enough to make Lex flinch. He gripped the edges of the door frame to stop himself from reaching out for her. "Anyway," she sighed again, "I'm giving you the courtesy you never gave me. I'm telling you to your face what I really think of you. You're despicable and I wish you hurt even half as much as I'm hurting now." Her lashes fluttered again and for a frozen moment, Lex thought she was going to cry. But she wiped a rough fist over her eyes. "*Jesus*, you two must have laughed your heads off at me. Pathetic Noelle thinking that a guy like Alexander the Snake would actually be into her."

Lex couldn't let her think that. "Please, don't—" He reached out, but she jerked away from him.

"I don't want any more lies." Then she turned and walked away from his doorstep, heading down the drive. Through the thunder of his swiftly pounding heart, Lex noticed the grimy bottoms of her feet, the empty driveway.

"Did you walk here?"

But she just kept walking, back straight, shoes swinging viciously in her tight grip. It was too late for her to be walking alone.

"Let me take you home," he said to her back. "It's not safe."

She swung to face him and snarled, the illusion of calm gone. Fresh tears lined the hollows of her eyes. "The idea of being trapped in a car with you makes me *sick*."

Her words kicked him in the stomach, and it was

only his tight grip on the edges of the door frame that kept him from running after her, begging her forgiveness, offering an explanation. But what explanation was there other than that he'd messed up?

"Let me…let me at least call you a taxi." He squeezed the words past his tight throat. "I'll pay the fare."

But she kept walking, and Lex watched her and the future he'd wanted with her disappear around the bend in his driveway while every sense told him to stop her any way he could. Not just because of the things he wanted very, very badly, but because it just wasn't safe.

What if something happened to her out there alone?

Worse than what you've done? an inner voice taunted.

Lex bit off a curse. In the kitchen, he quickly grabbed his keys and phone, shoved his feet into flip-flops by the door and chased after Noelle. Hurrying down the brightly lit drive, he used his phone to request an Uber pickup, glancing between the phone and his path to make sure he didn't bump into anything. It wasn't long before he got close enough to see her dark dress and hair, illuminated under streetlights and moving steadily away from him.

The street was empty, most cars long asleep in his quiet corner of suburbia. Noelle walked in the right direction toward her house, but, at this rate, she wouldn't get there until sunrise. Lex silently followed.

Minutes later, a silver Prius pulled up behind him the same time his phone rang.

"Hey, is this you walking up Miami Place?" A feminine voice, alert and cheerful for so late at night, chirped through the phone.

"Yeah, but the ride is not for me."

The glow of a cell phone in the Prius showed the driver, a youngish woman with short hair, peering through the windshield at him. Lex walked the short distance to the car, still talking with her on the phone. The woman eyed him with suspicion and it somehow made him feel better to see a Taser sitting in her passenger seat, her hand not very far from it.

Standing a few feet away from the car to make sure the woman felt safe, he gestured toward Noelle and hung up his phone. "Pick her up and take her to the address I gave or wherever she wants to go." He slipped the driver a few bills and took a quick photo of her just to be safe. Up ahead, Noelle looked over her shoulder at them but kept walking.

"I can do that." The driver put the money in her pocket, nodded and then eased the car toward Noelle.

Lex clenched his fists in his pockets and held his breath, hoping she wouldn't refuse the ride. But after a quick discussion he couldn't hear, Noelle got into the car. The Prius slowly drove away, leaving him with all his good intentions crumbled to dust in his clenched fists.

Lex released a breath through parted lips and turned to walk back home. With the taillights of the Prius only an afterimage and Noelle relatively safe, he couldn't stop thinking of other things. Like the chances he'd been given time and time again to make things right with Noelle. His wildness as a youth that had ultimately led him to this place.

When she'd left him at the pizza parlor, he had been in shock at how suddenly their paradise had withered. Just the night before, she'd bucked like a wild thing beneath him, clawing his back for release while desperate, needful noises vibrated in her throat. He had wanted to explain, to confess. But in the aftermath of his revealed past, he had felt the gates crash down between them.

In the morning, Lex had promised himself, he would tell her everything.

Now he would never get the chance.

Lex pulled out his phone and dialed a number he wished he'd never used. Margot picked up on the first ring. He had to swallow past the lump in his throat before he could talk. "Did you talk to Noelle?" he asked.

"Yes!" Margot sounded frantic, and that alone tightened the feeling of dread in his stomach. "She left my place hours ago. Did she call you? I've been driving around all night looking for her."

"Relax," Lex said, although he was one to talk. It felt like his pulse was about to punch its way through his neck. He wanted to chase after Noelle, beg her forgiveness, sit outside her house until she came outside and talked to him. "She came to see me at home."

"Thank God! Wait—she walked all that way?"

"Seems like it. I called for a car to take her home."

The silence on the other end of the phone was worse than Margot cursing. Then she said, "You were right. What I asked you to do wasn't…wasn't well thought-out. I should've stopped this long before it got to this point." The sound of unshed tears threaded through her voice. "She ran out of here two hours ago without her purse. Her car is still downstairs. She doesn't even have the keys to her house. I… I have to go…go let her into the house."

"She might not want to see you," Lex said, though

part of him knew Noelle would more easily forgive Margot than him. Margot was family, while he was… nobody. Just another man who'd lied to her.

"Well, sometimes we don't always get what we want." Margot's voice grew firm. "I'll talk with you later." Then she hung up.

For once, Lex tried to be patient. He waited an entire week before doing what he had wanted to do the moment the silver Prius disappeared with her in the backseat. His mother said patience was never his strong suit, but he willing to try it on for Noelle. She was right though—after a week of waiting he realized again what he had always known. Patience wasn't for him. A big part of strategy, he thought as he parked his car near Noelle's house late Tuesday night while she was at her dance class, was knowing when waiting was a losing game.

He walked the rest of the way to her front gate, mentally rehearsing what he would say. Wearing all black, Lex paced the length of her front yard and then the back, periodically checking his watch. This was about time for Noelle to have drinks with Malia and Ruby after their dance class. That gave him about a half hour to go over what he would tell Noelle to convince her not to throw him off her property. Lex closed the backyard gate, preparing himself to wait on the front porch when he heard the sound of cars pulling into the driveway. He froze.

Damn.

A tall, flowering bush mostly hid him from view, but it was only a matter of time before someone noticed him. He took a breath and walked fully into sight.

Noelle stepped out of her car first, gym bag over her shoulder and talking with Malia who climbed from the passenger side of the little Honda. "It's just cheaper," she was saying as Ruby came out of her own car. Ruby noticed him first, surprise registering on her face and then anger. "I can make drinks here and—" Noelle stopped when she noticed her friend gawking past her. She turned. Her hiss of surprise, the crack of pain across her face jerked Lex's spine upright.

He was very aware of how it looked. A liar dressed all in black, looking ready to do some more damage to the woman he'd deceived for the better part of three months. Acting on the nonchalance he did not feel, he shoved his hands in the pockets of his jeans and faced Noelle head-on.

"I didn't expect you back so soon," he said.

"Are you serious right now?" Ruby pushed past Noelle to confront him, pulling out her cell phone at the same time. Lex winced as she took a photo of him. "Trespassing is a crime," she hissed. "I'm damn sure she didn't give you permission to come here."

"You have a big set of brass ones on you," Malia said. She hid Noelle behind her, a protective mother hen of the type Margot never was, while Noelle stared at him like she was seeing a ghost.

Her mouth opened and then closed a few times before she spoke. "Get out of here!" she all but shouted, the sound of her voice like an open wound.

Lex didn't think he could feel any worse, but he was wrong. "I just want to talk with you for a few minutes," he told her softly, hating himself.

"That's why you're in my yard uninvited? To tell me

more lies?" Even though she was taller, Noelle huddled behind Malia, looking small and defenseless.

"I'm calling the cops." Ruby practically spat the words in his face.

Lex turned to Ruby, who was already furiously pressing buttons on her phone. "Don't do that." Noelle's pain, naked on her face, throbbed so deeply that he felt it like it was his own. "Please," he said to her. "Just listen. No more half-truths."

"Give me one damn reason why I shouldn't call!" Ruby waved her phone in his face, looking mad enough to actually call the cops and then hit him in the face with it once she was done.

But Lex kept his attention focused on Noelle. She was the one he needed to see more than anyone else. As he looked at her now, her face seemed drawn and worried, but for those few moments while she'd stood talking with her friends in the sun and before they saw him, she had actually looked if not happy, then at least okay. Like she wasn't going to break apart. As he was in danger of doing.

"What I did for Margot was stupid. But the things I said and did with you weren't lies." Lex held the next words in his mouth for a moment and then carefully released them. "I want you in my life for real, Noelle. If you'll have me."

"That's not a good enough reason," Ruby said, her fingers still on her phone.

"Girls, girls…" Noelle sounded tired. Done. "It's okay. I—" She gripped the strap of her gym bag tightly enough to show flexing bones and tendons just under the skin. "Lex, go get up under Margot, not me. You've done enough here. Please, just leave." Noelle moved toward the front door. She was walking away from him again.

"I love you."

All oxygen felt like it was suddenly sucked from the air. The three women stared at Lex while he squirmed, wishing he could take back his hastily spoken truth. Finally, Ruby was the one who spoke.

"This is the route you're going?" She jammed her phone into the pocket of her purse. "This woman trusted you with her healing self and with her body, but you still decided to trick and bamboozle her? Now you think you can fix everything with some cheesy rom-com declaration? Boy, get the hell outta here."

But Noelle stood frozen near the door leading to the sanctuary of her home. "How can that be true after what you've done?" she asked.

"I should've told you about my agreement with Margot long before this."

"How about you shouldn't have agreed to do that crap at all?" Ruby's gaze was pure anger. Lex had a strong feeling it was only Noelle's wounded expression that kept her from calling the police. But her wounds were his too. He'd done this thing to both of them and was ready to make it up to her any way he could.

"Noelle, can we just talk?" he asked, pitching his voice low to reveal some of the agony he felt. He hadn't been sleeping. His work suffered. Even Adisa was worried about him. "Please?"

Just steps away from her front door and escape from him, Noelle curled her hands around herself, rubbed her shoulders like she was cold. But there was something other than dismissal in her eyes. "You aren't too proud to beg?"

Lex nearly sagged with relief. "That wouldn't be my choice of words just now, but the sentiment is the same." If she was open enough to joke with him, then maybe he had a sliver of a chance.

"I can already see where this is going." Malia looked from Noelle to Lex and shook her head. "Ruby, we're about to be SOL with those margaritas."

Ruby clicked her tongue in disapproval the same moment Noelle stepped toward Lex. "Girls, can you give us a little time alone, please?"

"I want to go on record as saying this is not a good idea," Malia said.

Noelle bit her lip. "I know…but please understand."

Lex didn't know how the two women resisted that look of hers. Eyes wide, mouth vaguely trembling. Arms around herself like she needed protection and he was the only one who could provide it for her.

"All right, honey. If that's what you want." Ruby gave Noelle a quick hug and whispered something in her ear.

Malia glared at Lex with a viciousness he knew was meant to frighten, but it only made him glad Noelle had such loyal and protective friends. She put her hands on Noelle's shoulders. "Ruby and I will be at the gas station down the street. If you need us, just call. Okay?"

Noelle hugged her friends and thanked them, her voice a soft apology for breaking the plans they'd made.

"Get it together, Private Dancer," Ruby muttered to Lex as she passed him. "I was rooting for you. Don't mess up again and make me look like Boo Boo the Fool."

The two women climbed into Ruby's car and, after

waiting a longer time than Lex thought was necessary, they drove off. Then he and Noelle were alone.

With a slow hiss, Lex released the breath he'd been holding. "Thanks for not kicking me out," he said.

"Yet."

"Yet." Lex nodded and wet his lips, watched her warily, just as she watched him.

After a thoughtful pause, Noelle opened the front door and invited him in with a brusque wave. "Say what you have to, Lex. I need to shower."

He brushed close to her as he stepped into the house.

"You already showered," he said. He could smell her, the orange-blossom sweetness of the Caress soap she used mingled with after-bath shea butter and her own natural perfume. He remembered too well the entwined scents where they lay intimately against her skin, in the crook of her elbow, the back of her neck, between her thighs.

Noelle dipped her head, a subtle flush rising in her cheeks as if she knew where his mind had gone, as if her own mind roamed the same path. She dropped her gym bag by the front door and then backed away to perch at the entrance to the hallway leading to her bedroom and that shower she didn't need.

Lex took a mental step back. If he lingered any more on what she smelled like, their discussion would be over before it properly started. He cleared his throat. "I never faked what I feel for you."

He allowed the present tense to seep into her, into him. This was damn near the first time he fully admitted it to himself. The more-than-lust he felt for Noelle. Wanting her was effortless. What surprised him were the ropes of affection that began tying him to her not

long after their first day together. Feelings that had
nothing to do with a booty call and everything to do
with a woman he could see in his life for a very long
time.

"I don't want to believe that," Noelle said. "Not after
everything." She hovered near the hallway still, un-
committed. Her body was in the room with him but
ready to flee if he said the wrong thing. "You made
me think you and I wanted the same things. You built
such an ache in me that I couldn't feel the breeze on
my skin without wanting to touch you. You made me
think you were for me." She confronted him with her
eyes and the naked pain in them.

For me.

Those were the words that caught him and held him
brutally accountable. Nothing would change the fact
that he'd allowed himself to be used as a puppet and a
weapon against her. Even if the intent hadn't been ma-
licious. Once, she'd thought he was the only thing in
her life that her sister hadn't deliberately manipulated
into it. Once. Now, only complete truth gave him any
chance of rescuing his future with her.

"When I saw you that night at the gallery, I wanted
you."

Noelle blinked and swung her gaze to him, his new
tack unexpected to them both. But since it felt right,
Lex continued on.

"The celibacy thing was new to me. And when I saw
you, not five seconds after I had told my brother I'd
sworn off sex for a while, I wanted to kiss you.

"I wanted to follow you around the room and give
you my number, convince you to come home with me
and let me worship your body all night. But I said the

stupid thing about being celibate and my brother was right there." He drew a deep breath and brought himself back from the past. "I was yours then, and I'm yours now."

The room's silence felt heavy after his confession died away, and Lex felt his stomach drop. Had he said the wrong thing? But the air near him shifted and Noelle moved past him to sit on the couch with her hands clasped in her lap. He took the armchair across from her.

With her head bowed, she nibbled the corner of her lip for long moments before meeting his eyes. "I'm telling you this for the last time," she said. "I don't like games."

A breath of relief left his lips with a huff. "I know."

"I couldn't take it if you—"

"I know. I won't."

Noelle nodded. "Okay then."

And Lex felt for the first time that miracles actually existed. Like wings had sprung from somewhere and saved him from his own foolhardy step off a high cliff. He felt breathless. Dizzy with happiness. Even though fifteen feet of space separated him from Noelle, they were finally together in the way they were meant to be. A grin split his face wide and made him feel like a clown. He sang the opening bars of "Up Where We Belong" in a falsetto that was nothing like Jennifer Warnes's voice. A pillow flew across the room and hit him in the face.

"Are you sure about this?" Noelle used the excuse of checking her lipstick one more time to disguise her nervousness. But she had a feeling the only person she fooled was herself.

Lex sat in the driver's seat of the big car, his thighs sprawled comfortably wide, arm draped across the back of her seat like he had all night to wait for her despite the circular driveway being full of cars and the fact that the last person to arrive had already gone into the massive house nearly fifteen minutes before.

"I'm sure," he said. "I'm the one who invited you, remember?"

"Invited *us*, you mean."

A smile thinned his lips. "Yes." His fingers brushed her shoulders, a light caress that stirred a familiar flutter of desire in her belly despite her anxiety.

"Speaking of which…"

A familiar black Benz pulled up behind them. Only a few seconds passed before the driver got out of the car, locked the door with a chirp of the remote and began the long walk toward the front veranda of the large Spanish-style house.

"Come on," Lex said. "We can't let her go in by herself."

"Okay." Noelle pressed her lips together, less to even out her lipstick than to calm her breaths. "Let's go."

She opened the car door and the interior light flashing on made the figure rushing toward the house pause, turn around and then wait for Noelle and Lex to come closer.

"I thought you would already be in there," Margot said.

She looked almost casual in her skinny jeans and high heels. But the leather blazer killed casual before it had a chance to properly live.

Lex gave her a once-over, chuckling dryly. "You look like you're ready for a corporate takeover, not to meet my family."

"There are similar principles in both," Margot said.

Smiling, he shook his head but didn't overtly disagree. Noelle hung back slightly behind him. She wasn't quite back to the point of joking with her sister (had she ever really been there?), but they were talking again and Lex seemed as comfortable around her as he did anyone else. Family was family. Despite the things other than love that came with it. She couldn't shut Margot out of her life and, to be honest, she didn't want to. They had boundaries now and Margot knew not to cross them.

"I hope we're not going to stand here looking at each other all night," Lex said, giving both her and Margot a prodding glance. "I'm starving."

Noelle forced a smile. "Okay. Let's go meet the Diallos then."

At the front door of what Noelle would politely call a mansion, Lex used a key to let them in and, instantly, they were surrounded by the most amazing food smells Noelle had ever experienced. The inside of the house wasn't bad either, dark and polished wood, a spiral staircase in the foyer leading up and light spilling from everywhere. The smell of good food merged with the sounds of laughter and dozens of voices in conversation, interlaced with old-time reggae music.

"I think I love your family already." She squeezed Lex's elbow and he grinned down at her.

"Mission accomplished," he said. "We can go home now."

Margot was quiet on Lex's other side, just watching

their interaction with warmth in her eyes. That, more than anything, had brought Noelle close to her sister again—Margot's genuine happiness for her and Lex.

"Alexander, is that you?" A warm female voice called out from inside the house.

Before he could answer, a slim form came through the foyer, high heels tapping against the hardwoods, hips swinging in a pink tutu-style dress. Adisa. "Of course it's him, Mama!" Lex's twin tossed over her shoulder as she hugged her brother tight.

"Lexie!" Adisa threw her arms around her brother while Margot looked past them at Noelle.

Lexie? She mouthed the question with a faint smile. Noelle shrugged. This nickname was news to her too.

Then she was being pulled into a warm hug and enfolded in the scent of an expensive citrus perfume.

"Success!" Adisa said, pulling back with a wild grin. "I'm glad he finally seduced you into the family."

"This is family dinner, not a wedding, Adisa." Lex plucked at his sister's neck with teasing fingers.

"You've never brought a woman home to meet us so it's practically the same thing." Adisa moved on to Margot, giving her a similar hug despite the tight look on her face.

Noelle hid a smile behind the back of her hand. "This is my sister, Margot."

"A pleasure!" She squeezed Margot's waist at the tail end of the hug like they were already friends. "Come meet everyone."

Everyone turned out to be nearly as effusive as Adisa, pulling Noelle into warm hugs and welcoming her to her first family dinner.

The names came at her quickly, but every time she

talked to one of the brothers or sisters, she said their names a couple of times and looked them in the eye to help her remember. Wolfe, Nichelle, Kingsley, Carter, Elia, Jaxon, Paxton, Lola.

Their parents were gorgeous. Noelle instantly fell in love with how they seemed to adore each other. Teasing and casually touching, exchanging speaking looks that seemed like a language that had developed between companions over time. Lex's mother, tall and elegant in a poppy-colored sundress. Her husband, casually handsome in slacks and a guayabera.

Once Noelle had met everyone, Alice pulled her into the kitchen to break a food-tasting tie, which was only necessary because their mother had gone into a frenzy of cooking and accidentally made two batches of oxtail from two different recipes. They couldn't decide which to put out with dinner. Noelle tasted the recipes and fell in love with both, not wanting to choose one or the other. Alice congratulated her on her good taste and took both platters out to the dining room table.

It all felt warm and cozy. Welcoming. When Noelle caught Margot's gaze across the room, she knew her sister was feeling the same.

Dinner was beautiful chaos. Laughter and stories and Lex touching her knee in reassurance under the table.

After the meal, Noelle was full to bursting. When she tried to help clear the table, Kingsley waved her off to go find Lex. She wandered through the elegant house, got caught up with admiring its furnishings, the paintings on the walls, landscape oils of Jamaica, portraits of Lex's grandparents, who had arrived from Jamaica on separate boats back in the 1940s. The house was large but warm, filled with the smells and sounds that made it feel intimate like a family lived and loved there. And the spiral staircase was stunning. The wood warmed quickly under her hand, seeming to snuggle into her palm like an animal wanting to be petted.

"I don't want you to be angry."

She stopped when she heard Lex's voice, realizing she had walked all the way upstairs and was now at the opening of a long and wide hallway. This conversation seemed like something she didn't need to hear. But the ache in Lex's voice kept her feet firmly planted.

"Why would we be angry?" His mother's voice, soft and accented, floated closer.

Silence pulsed from the room.

"Tell us, Alexander. What is on your mind?" His father's voice rumbled deep with affection.

More silence. Shifting cloth. "I like it in this family. I don't want to be disowned." Lex's humor seemed forced. Noelle bit her lip, gripping the banister to stop herself from going to him.

"If you don't say what's on your mind…"

Someone sighed. "I took my clothes off for money when you sent me to Jamaica." The words came out in a rush, low but clear before silence rushed into the room again.

"That's it?" his mother asked many heartbeats later.

"Why would we disown you for something we already know?"

"What?"

Noelle pressed her fingers to her mouth. Lex had been terrified of telling them, swearing up and down that his parents would hide him away from the public for a while or do something equally terrible. But he'd been determined to give them all of the truth and stop deceiving the people he loved.

"You knew? For how long?"

"Probably for most of the time you did it," his mother said. "You probably forgot how small the island is, and the city."

"What…" Noelle could almost imagine the look on Lex's face. Amazement and irritation. Relief.

She smiled. Then she turned to go back downstairs. She drew a sharp breath when the wooden floor creaked under her feet.

Damn.

She grabbed the banister and kept going only to hear movement behind her.

"Noelle?" Lex peered at her.

"I'll just meet you downstairs," she said and then walked quickly away to allow him some semblance of privacy.

But he followed and pulled her out to the porch where a couple rocked together in one hammock. He coaxed her down a dimly lit path to a garden sweet with the scent of peonies. The grass sucked at her high heels before Lex pulled her onto a stone path and into a small gazebo glowing pale under the quarter moon.

"Did you hear everything?" He was breathing fast, the skin in the open neck of his T-shirt clammy under her palms.

"Not everything but enough," Noelle said. "You're really lucky. Your parents are incredible." But she knew the shock he felt after keeping what he thought was a ten-year-old secret only to find out that it…wasn't.

She consciously steered her thoughts away from her own parents and how they'd abandoned her and Margot to a life defined by sacrifice. To have parents like Hyacinth and Glendon Diallo was a windfall Noelle couldn't even imagine. They loved their children, and they cared for them.

Lex made a sound that was like pain. "I can't believe I…"

She gripped his shoulders to get his attention. "The past is over. Isn't that what you always tell me? They love you. They've always accepted you, no matter what."

She slid a hand up to cup his jaw. "Just like I love and accept you."

He dropped back against the sturdy gazebo wall, his face incredulous under the moon's faint light. "Yeah?"

"Yeah. I wouldn't be here with your whole family otherwise."

His breath, layered with a hint of red wine, brushed her cheek. He pressed their foreheads together and stroked a warm hand up the back of her neck.

"I'm the luckiest man alive," Lex whispered.

"I'm the one who's lucky," Noelle said, feeling for the first time in her life that she truly was.

* * * * *

REQUEST YOUR FREE BOOKS!

2 FREE NOVELS PLUS 2 FREE GIFTS!

KIMANI™
ROMANCE

Love's ultimate destination!

JUST CAN'T GET ENOUGH?

Join our social communities
and talk to us online.

You will have access to the latest
news on upcoming titles and special
promotions, but most importantly,
you can talk to other fans about your
favorite Harlequin reads.

Harlequin.com/Community

Facebook.com/HarlequinBooks

Twitter.com/HarlequinBooks

Pinterest.com/HarlequinBooks

Everything schoolteacher Morgan Hill loves is in her hometown of Temptation, Virginia—her twins, her students and the charming community center where she's staging their holiday play. But now the building's new owner, Grayson Taylor, is putting sexy visions into Morgan's head, making the young widow long for a future even Santa couldn't deliver...

Read on for a sneak peek at
ONE MISTLETOE WISH,
the first exciting installment in author A.C. Arthur's
TAYLORS OF TEMPTATION *series!*

Her back was to the window and Gray moved to stand in front of her. He rubbed the backs of his fingers lightly over her cheek.

"Those buildings mean something to you, don't they?" he asked her.

She shrugged, shifting from one foot to the other as if his proximity was making her nervous. Being this close to her was making him hot and aroused. He wondered if that was what she was really feeling, as well.

"This town means something to me. There are good people here and we're trying to do good things."

"That's what my mother used to say," Gray continued, loving the feel of her smooth skin beneath his touch. "Temptation was a good place. Love, family, loyalty. They meant something to the town. Always. That's what she used to tell us when we were young. But that was after the show, after my father found something better outside of this precious town of Temptation."

Gray could hear the sting to his tone, felt the tensing of his muscles that came each time he thought about Theodor Taylor and all that he'd done to his family. Yes, Gray had buried his father two months ago. He'd followed the old man's wishes right down to the ornate gold handles on the slate-gray casket, but Gray still hated him. He still despised any man that could walk away from his family without ever looking back.

"Show me something better," he found himself saying as he stared down into Morgan's light brown eyes. "Show me what this town is really about and maybe I'll reconsider selling."

"Are you making a bargain with me?" she asked. "Because if you are, I don't know what to say. I'm not used to wheeling and dealing big businessmen like you."

"I'm asking you to give me a reason why I shouldn't sell those buildings. Just one will do. If you can convince me—"

She was already shaking her head. "I won't sleep with you, if that's what you mean by *convince* you."

Don't miss ONE MISTLETOE WISH
by A.C. Arthur, available December 2016
wherever Harlequin® Kimani Romance™
books and ebooks are sold.